A SHIP CALLED EROS

Mark Tungesvik MD

BOOK TWO OF THE NARROW PATH SERIES

S^AHIP
CALLED
EROS

*To my friends who have found courage in the face of
adversity and have chosen to live this life to the fullest*

Contents

CHAPTER 1

DARK REFLECTIONS

AD 6

A COOL DESERT WIND pulled the linen robe tight against Xaphan's back. The tattered cloth slapped his chest like whips on a horse that had seen one too many battles. From an outcropping of rock, he looked upon his reflection in a pool of water and studied his torn wings, singed from wars long past. He rubbed his hand across one of the ragged feathers, trying to remember how they had looked before the rebellion. His heart filled with rage. He turned toward his brother, Tarat.

"This broken image was not of my choosing. It's yet another shackle from the one who controls all things with his magical song. It is just another form of control. Is this not why we rebelled? To be captains of our own ship? To create reality as *we* see fit?"

Tarat nodded. "It's too dangerous to keep this form, Xaphan. The legions of angels loyal to him will hunt you down. They know your shape from afar—even your scent. It's bad enough being hunted by those beasts that sprang into existence with the curse on the man. You're the last to hold the old form. Let it go."

Xaphan pulled his hand from his tattered wing and nodded. "So be it. I'll recreate myself as I see fit and release the last shackle of his oppressive creation." Xaphan then held his hands high in the air and shouted his real name—the one that must never be uttered. His form shivered at the sound that defined it to its core. He then began to sing a dark song of scales and wings and long talons. With each angelic word, his form grew and shifted.

Across the pool arose the reflection of a giant dragon. With each word, spikes erupted out of his head and at the edge of his wings. Xaphan took in a deep breath and then blew a stream of fire over the pool, lighting the surrounding desert up as if it were day. He then looked over to Tarat, who was in the form of a white panther. "Now his legions will see me as one of those beasts created by the curse. Do you think that Kytan's plan will work? Our oppressor's magic runs deep. Things have not gone well for us thus far."

"Kytan said the magic is in his blood. We have but to harness that magic and form a weapon strong enough to kill him."

Xaphan nodded. "Kill him with his own magic. But why not just rub the blood on a sword and kill him with that?"

Tarat leaned in close. "The power of the magic must infuse the thing and grow. We must put the blood on the seeds of the black trees and let them grow. Then we can cut weapons from them that will be strong with his power. Then we will kill him."

Xaphan looked out at the dark pool. "What of the legions of angels that protect him now that he has come down in the form of a man?"

Tarat jumped up, waving his paws in the air. "The weapons will be unstoppable. We will cut them down like grass. Then it will be like it was before we were thrown down from the high heavens."

Xaphan nodded. "Except we will be in charge of our own reality. We will recreate this world as we see fit."

"What do you think will become of mankind?"

"They'll need to go. They remind me too much of him." Behind them a bush rustled, and Xaphan turned in the blink of an eye, ready to blow fire on whomever approached.

Kytan stood before them in the form of a giant wolf. His eyes grew cross at the sight of Xaphan. "Why have you taken the shape of a dragon? Could you not find a less conspicuous form to wander the earth?"

Xaphan smiled as he ran a claw down the smooth scales of his neck. "Splendid, isn't it? It's the first time I've felt free to be myself since we were driven from the upper heavens to be exiled on this filthy rock." He then pointed a wagging claw at Kytan. "And don't lecture me about my form. You chose to run around in the form of a wolf the size of an elephant. Neither of us can walk freely in the light of day." He then leaned in closer to Kytan. "Do you think they know?"

Kytan turned his head toward the horizon. "There would be a legion of his angels around us if they knew."

Xaphan stretched his neck to get a closer look at the wolf. Kytan held out his paw, revealing six black seeds. With great delicacy, he squeezed out the tiniest drop of blood from a mosquito that had bitten his nemesis. He carefully coated each of the seeds with that precious blood, looking left and right apprehensively.

Kytan held one of the seeds to give to Xaphan. The dragon took the seed and brought it close to his eye. "Is that it? I expected fire and smoke and some sort of thunderous noise. This looks like just another ordinary seed."

Kytan smiled. "Take care where you plant it so that it will not be seen by the world of men or angels. It needs time to grow."

Xaphan tucked the seed under one of his scales. "I know my role in this little play of ours. I have the perfect place in mind. I will seek you out when the tree has grown and I have fashioned a weapon from it."

With that Xaphan took flight. In the distance he could see Tarat bounding across the desert toward a distant mountain range. He flew hard through the night to a remote island in the middle of the ocean. At its highest peak lay the opening to a volcano. He perched on the rim of the crater and looked down at the vast city that lay far below on the shores of the island. It was a great city of men that had secluded themselves from the world and created a culture that surpassed anything he had witnessed in his travels. They were the best of their kind. They too would have to go, of course. But the time for that had not yet come. In the meantime, he had a project that they would fit in perfectly with.

With that thought, Xaphan dropped the seed into the middle of the crater. He did not hear it hit bottom, but he knew that it took root as soon as it hit the soil far below. The mountain shook fiercely, with large rocks rolling down its side. Xaphan took flight, fearful that the volcano would erupt. While he was high in the sky, he caught a glimpse of what looked like a white bear emerging from the waves on the distant horizon. In his heart he knew that what he saw was related to the evil he had just planted, but he did not know how. He then turned his attention back to the city. He could wait for the war to be won before reshaping reality as he saw fit—but why? That could take a long time. He would start to reform reality on this island here and now. He would have to be crafty to make it work. He had just the plan. He then flew straight down into the volcano's crater. Out of the corner of his eye, just before he passed out of sight, he again caught the image of the white bear on the distant waves.

He shuddered.

CHAPTER 2

TREACHERY IN PARADISE

One thousand years later

FLAN, A MAN WITH the hind legs of a panther, stood still as his eyes passed down a scroll that hung to his paws. Written in pure gold were Xaphan's instructions for the daily decoration of the palace, as well as the allotted times for his administrative functions. He paused for a moment and gazed across the great golden hall that had been built in the crater of the volcano. Servants bounded about, setting out fresh flowers and resetting the tapestries. Flan remembered how they had once been. Some were still mostly human; others had features mostly of beasts, with only their eyes revealing their human origin. Each was designed for the role they played in the running of the palace. Flan's role was to ensure that things went according to the plan. He looked over to the far end of the golden cave. Bright red and purple cloths were being delicately laid out on hundreds of pillows laced with silk and satin fringe, where Xaphan would soon sit after his morning swim in the sea. The sound of great wings flapping sounded overhead. The man clapped his hands. Everyone finished what they were doing and disappeared into the hallways that riddled the golden hall.

* * * * *

Xaphan looked down at the crater that was now his home. He had come to enjoy his current status as a local deity. He circled once overhead so that all in the city far below could see his beautiful wet scales shimmer in the morning light and then dove into the deep crater below, landing next to the resting place that had been prepared for him. He looked around the hall for imperfections, but there were none. The hall gleamed with gold, covered with tapestries of purple, the color he had declared for today. A smile crept onto his face as he looked down at his servant holding the ledger.

"Flan, what do you have in store for me today?"

Flan flipped to the second page and looked up. "While inspecting all temples in the city to ensure that all sculptures and paintings of you accurately reflect your beauty in accordance with your edict, we found an outlier."

Xaphan raised the scales above one eye. "Their artists were not skilled in rendering my form?"

Flan kept his eyes on the ledger. "Their artists were not making images of you. They were rendering works depicting a white bear."

Xaphan's neck stiffened as his eyes glowed bright red. "They had artwork depicting the sea bear in one of my temples?"

Flan shook his head, still not making eye contact. "It was not one of your temples. It was a temple erected for the white bear."

Fire streamed from Xaphan's mouth down through the middle of the hall toward the black tree that stood at the opposite end of the golden cave. "That cult was eradicated one hundred years ago. Look at all the beauty I have infused into their culture." Xaphan waved his claw toward the tapestries of half-humans. "What more could they want?"

The man looked up and nodded. "You have been very generous."

"I only ask my due—that they worship me as their creator." He looked down at Flan. "You enjoy your panther legs, don't you?"

The man shook one of his legs. "Immensely, great Xaphan. But some have refused the operation. Some in the city remain fully human." The man lowered his voice. "They claim they were created by the bear the way they are and that to change their form would be an insult to him."

Xaphan looked up at the cave's golden ceiling and blew a stream of fire that melted a portion of the gold, causing molten raindrops of gold to fall near the man. "This worship of the bear must be stopped."

Flan rubbed a burn mark on his arm. "We've brought the head priestess of the bear temple to you today, great Xaphan, for your judgment." The man clapped his hands, and men that were fused with the body of a horse at the torso brought in a woman dressed in white linen. Her hands and feet were bound in chains.

The dragon examined her thoughtfully for several minutes before he spoke. "Captain, this is one of my subjects. Remove her chains."

One of the horse men trotted up to her and unlocked her chains. He cringed as his hands touched her, as if he would become infected.

Xaphan waved his claw toward the guards. They turned and left.

When they were out of hearing range, Xaphan lowered his head toward Solara's face so he could see into her eyes.

"What do you think you are worshiping when you worship the sea bear?"

Solara did not so much as flinch as she replied. "The white bear created all things and keeps them in existence through the power of his song. We were created by him to care for his creation."

Xaphan nodded. "I see … and you have met this bear?"

"I've seen him in my dreams."

Xaphan rubbed one of his claws on a scale below his chin. "Dreams can be tricky things." He then pulled his head away. "Unlike you, I have met your bear—or, more accurately, the one you identify as a bear—and you are correct that he created you and that his magic runs deep through the song he sings."

Solara took a step toward the dragon. "I thought that you denied the existence of the bear. This is what is said in your temples."

Xaphan looked away. "It is a complicated subject. You know only what he has revealed to you in dreams. I have known him for thousands of years. I know more of him than you could imagine." Xaphan then stood tall and walked toward a massive opening to his left.

"Come walk with me, and I will tell you of him and show you my underground city."

Xaphan began to walk toward the opening and, without looking back, waved his claw for the woman to follow. As they entered the darkness of the tunnel, he spoke.

"In times before this world was created I served the one you call the bear. He claimed to have created us, as he now does with you. My kind were far more beautiful and powerful than yours. We served him for eons until some of our kind found a deeper truth—the truth

7

that the song that sustains all things is itself self-sustaining. It is not dependent on the one you call the bear. He has deep magic that can control it, but it is not dependent on him."

Xaphan looked down at Solara and could see in her eyes that she did not believe him. He smiled and shook his head. In a way, she represented all of humanity to him—beings walking in the dark. "Your short life is like that of a flower that blooms once in the field, and the universe is far vaster than your mind can comprehend. Your capacity to make any decisions on your own is folly. We, on the other hand, have seen the universe from its beginning. We have watched it over countless years. It is too vast and too complex for the one you know as the bear to hold it together with his song. It was observation and reason that led us to our new knowledge. It was either that or trust in his account of how things are created and maintained. We choose to trust reason over the word of our nemesis. We even taught a simplified version of this to truth to men long ago—a vision of solid matter that is self-sustaining. It is a ludicrous concept if you have seen the song at work, but it was too difficult to explain the concept of reality being created moment by moment by a master song. But we have digressed … Where were we? Oh yes, we had discovered a new truth that changed everything.

"Once we knew this one thing, we rightly questioned why we should not be allowed to create our own reality. Why should we be restricted to his version of reality? It's a question of dignity. We are great in our own right. Why should we bow to any authority? This line of thought was not well received. We therefore rightly rebelled … but his magic was too great and he and the angels that were loyal to him threw us from the light into this world you call home."

Xaphan noticed that the woman walked with confidence in the dark cave. She turned to him and said, "When the bear is within me, I feel serenity … I feel satisfied. A feeling of peace washes through my body. All that he has told me has come to be. This is what I know."

Xaphan nudged her to the right, where the dark tunnel opened up into a massive underground city. "This is the city that I built for my most loyal followers. Instead of lighting it with a sun that burns, I light it with rocks that glow." Xaphan waved his claw toward the sky where huge, glowing stalactites hung from the cave's ceiling. "Here there are no storms, no sweltering heat, no biting cold. It is a paradise on earth—an earth of my making."

The woman looked around her. "It's dark."

Xaphan looked down at her with a hint of surprise on his face. "Well … yesss … with respect to the outer world, it is darker by comparison." He then waved his claw to the hybrid people walking about on the street. Some were half-horse like the guards that had brought Solara to Xaphan, but the variety was endless. Some torsos had been placed on tall animals; others, on small animals. On some the only thing that was human was the head.

"All those here have been allowed to change their personal reality as they see fit. Their forms are now what they have chosen, as opposed to what they were given." Xaphan smiled as he looked out upon the city.

A man fused onto the body of a massive snake slithered by. Solara stepped back in revulsion. "By what power have all these people been changed?"

Xaphan looked down at the woman and smiled. "A very probing question. Let us continue to walk, and I will show you a thing very few in this world have ever seen."

The dragon then led her into another dark tunnel. "A long time ago I planted the black tree you noticed in my palace. Its seed was soaked in the blood of the one known to you as the bear. Our intention was to fashion a weapon from it to kill the bear, but to our surprise, he let your kind kill him." Xaphan looked down at the woman in the dark. "Does that surprise you?"

"I saw his death in a dream." Solara said.

"Yes … well … that does not surprise me. Now, where was I … oh yes. He died. I was, of course, elated. For three days we celebrated our freedom, and then something happened that I still do not fully understand. We saw that he was dead, and then three days later he was walking around speaking to people. As you can imagine, this was quite frustrating. But that was not the worst of it. He unleashed a power into this world—a magic deeper than we had yet seen. It drove us all into hiding. Anyway, it was clear to me that the dark weapon I had fashioned from the black tree was not going to defeat him. But I did find a use for it. It turns out that if you cut a man or an animal in half with the blade of the weapon, the man or beast does not die. And if you put the top of a man on the bottom of an animal after cutting them both with the blade, they fuse together. I discovered this quite by accident. I was quite elated."

The dragon and Solara turned a corner in the dark hall, and the tunnel widened into another massive opening. This time instead of a city there stood a giant pyramid with a black cube to its side.

Xaphan waved his claw in the air toward the pyramid. "This is where I celebrate all that I have created. Only my most loyal followers are allowed into this room. It is here that I have recorded the history of all that I have done."

The two walked toward the pyramid. As they approached, it became clear that there were steps leading up to the top of the pyramid. Lining those steps were statues that went up about two thirds the height of the structure. Once they arrived, the woman examined the lowest statue on the stairs with a quizzical look.

Xaphan ran a claw over the golden image. "This is how I found them: a man wanting to be a woman; a woman, a man. They rejected the reality that was given to them and yearned to create their own reality. I did not even put the thought in their head. But since they are not angelic, they did not have the power to truly change their own reality. They were forced to create a pretend reality in their minds and then act it out. They never really escaped the reality of the one you call the bear. They sought freedom as we did, but ironically, in doing so they built a prison in their minds. They could only pretend. I must admit that … against my better judgment … I felt a kindred spirit with them and their pretend rebellion."

Xaphan walked Solara up the stairs a bit. "What they could only pretend to do, I could do with a few lyrical words. I made men women and women men. It gave me some pleasure in knowing I was violating the intent of their creation. Once a rebel, always a rebel, I guess. Their yearnings were far too limited though. Why they focused on their gender so much puzzled me at first. If you are willing to create an entirely new reality, all that you can think of is modifying a few body parts? I didn't come upon the answer at first."

Xaphan bent down to take a closer look at a statue of a man that had been changed into a woman and ran his claw down the statue's back. "They were never happy after the change. Oh, there were several weeks of frolicking around in a new body, but after the newness wore off, they settled into a deep depression. Many of them took their own lives. At first I thought it had something to do with the song I had used to change them. I modified it time after time. Later it occurred to me that perhaps it was the society at large that was not accepting them. For many generations I modified their cultural norms through my temples ... but it did not help. Oddly enough, I noticed that those whom I had not yet changed but were still pretending were happier than anyone that I had ever changed. After experimenting with twenty generations of your kind, the answer finally came to me. What they were seeking was not really gender change at all; it was rebellion. They did not know it, of course. Once I gave them what they wanted, they realized that it was not what their hearts truly hungered for. Instead of basking in their own rebellious act, they felt empty. It is like a disease for your kind—to be driven to rebel and yet be driven mad when you achieve your end. They needed some help. They were thinking too small. I taught them to think big. It was then that we began experimenting with the dark blade."

As they continued up the stairs, they passed by statues of man and beast fused together. Xaphan ran his claw over the statues as they passed them. "Once we got started, there was no end to the combinations we could make. I even modified some of the animals so that their bodies would be large enough to fuse onto a human torso. But I kept running into the same problem. If I gave them everything they wanted, all at once they became depressed ... realizing that what they thought would make them happy was really not what they wanted at all."

Xaphan took her up higher on the stairs. He waved a claw at a likeness of a man with the legs of a great cat. "Look closely at his face."

Solara leaned in and then pulled back. "He is all cat. His nose and his mouth are not right."

Xaphan snorted a small cloud of smoke. "He is quite right. I changed him over the course of sixty years. It was an eloquent solution to an unsolvable problem. Your kind seeks perpetual change as a form of a never-ending rebellion. I put into his mind an unobtainable image of himself, and over the course of his short life I slowly tweaked him closer to his goal. The form I chose for them was almost irrelevant. It was the capacity to be in a perpetual state of rebellion that they really yearned for. The only thing that I asked in return was that they should worship me as their god. Which they were only too willing to do. After all, I was … in a sense … their creator."

Xaphan then smiled as if in a dream. "Just for fun, I even took some sea creatures and made them into monstrous things. It was a wonderful time for me. I let my creativity run wild. But as with all things, it too got a little old."

As they neared the top, the statues stopped. "I left this area open for future creations. At the very top, I will place a life-size likeness of myself."

As they reached the top, the woman looked across the upper platform and smiled. "It looks as though your worshipers had different plans for the top."

Xaphan looked across the top of his pyramid to find a giant likeness of the black tree sitting on the very center of the platform. Smoke rolled from his nostrils as his eyes glowed a bright red. He bounded over to the likeness of the tree, snatched it with his mouth, and ripped it out of the golden floor on which it sat. He threw it far away from the pyramid and then raised his head high and howled a terrible and broken cry. He then bounded back to the woman, who stood her ground.

"Traitors! After all that I have done for them, they dare to turn their back on me and worship the likeness of a tree? A *tree?* I created them! They owe me their very existence. They will pay dearly for this insult. Every last one of them." Xaphan then leaned down so that his face was right in front of the woman's. "Did your bear tell you of this treason?"

"No. But he asked me to tell you something."

Xaphan stepped back for a moment. "A message? For me? What did the bear say?"

"He said to tell you that he has seen the atrocities you have committed. He said that your time is coming to an end. He said that for you there would be no mercy."

Xaphan cringed as his eyes glowed red. "Did the bear tell you that you would die delivering this message?"

Solara looked into Xaphan's eyes with no fear in her own. "He said I would see him before the sun set today."

Xaphan's wings spread wide and his chest ballooned as he took in a deep breath. Before he exhaled, he saw a sublime smile on the woman's face. It showed a peace that he once knew many years ago—a peace his heart greatly desired. He then blew a stream of fire over and through the woman, reducing her to ash. Xaphan looked down at the pile of ash. "Say hello for me." He then broke into a nervous laugh and took off like the wind back toward his palace.

The great dragon burst into the palace room with his wings fully spread. He flew to the black tree, which was now nearly ten times his own height. "I will not share my glory with a mere *tree!* Your usefulness has now reached its end." And with that Xaphan took in a great breath and blew a torrent of fire through the black tree.

The dark wood immediately took to the flame. Fire soon engulfed the entire tree, but it did not diminish. It was then that the ground began to shake as if the entire mountain were angry.

Xaphan looked around at the shaking walls, and with fear in his heart he took flight out of the volcano. Hovering above the mountain, he watched the island violently shake as it began to sink into the ocean. The great city of men near the shore far below was swallowed by the sea in seconds. As the mountainous island descended, its peaks pulled apart. Xaphan watched in horror as his home crumbled down toward the ocean. Then, as quickly as it had begun, it stopped. What was once one giant island was now five smaller islands separated by sheer cliffs where they had split away from each other.

Xaphan looked down upon the small mountain outpost where they had captured the woman from the temple of the bear. The waves of the sea now covered a high plateau, licking up to the very edge of the buildings. He had just taken a great breath, intent on burning all that was left, when a cloud of ash erupted from the mountain below, engulfing him in its path. His mind became numb for a moment, as he imagined himself to be master of all things, including the fiery tree. He dove down through the ash into a pocket of clean air. His head suddenly cleared, and he hovered in the pocket of fresh air just to the side of the tree. As he stared at the tree, he tried to process what had just happened to him. It was as if his deepest desire had become a reality in his mind. The tree then began to quiver in the heat. At first he took it to be an illusion caused by the hot air, but then, to Xaphan's astonishment, what looked like silver birds began to emerge out of its bark by the thousands. They swarmed as if disorientated at first and then began to organize into a tight formation like a school of fish. Several moments passed before he realized that a juggernaut of silver birds was heading straight at him.

The dragon blew his pent-up fire at the birds, scattering them momentarily, but he did not fell a single bird. Several of the birds that had flown wide of his flame darted straight at him. Their speed was dizzying. Xaphan pulled up his wing to find five holes where they had pierced him. He looked up to find that the stray birds were now making an arc for another pass at him. He lunged hard to the right, evading four, but the fifth found his mark, piercing straight through the dragon, missing his heart by only inches.

Xaphan looked down upon the brood of gathering silver birds below and made off over the sea. As he passed over the small outpost by the sea, he saw a cloud of ash slowly fall down upon it like snow. This was the same ash that had nearly driven him mad. He considered doubling back and laying waste to those loyal to the bear, but as he watched the ash descend upon them, he thought better of it. He would let them languish in the ash. What madness would it induce in men if it could sway his mind so easily? He smiled as he contemplated watching its effects. He would need to wait, though. Better to let the tree and its silver dart birds calm down before returning to his palace. His mind then turned back to the statue of the tree on his pyramid. There was vengeance that needed to be meted out still … but how? His keen eye then spotted a small fire lizard swimming to shore from the carnage below. Xaphan smiled. The plan that was forming in his mind would take time. But time was one thing he had plenty of.

CHAPTER 3

NEW BEGINNINGS

Six centuries later

RAVEN STOOD IN A room covered with a thin layer of ash. On shelves she could see models of birds that she had put together as a child. There was a freedom about them that infatuated her—a freedom that she could never hope to ever find if she stayed here. It had now been a month since her mother had died. She had died from a disease that had no name. Her body wasted away to skin and bones in a little less than a year. It was the same strange illness her father had died of two years earlier. A lifetime of memories now lay in front of her, covered with the ash. She wished she could retreat into a private reality of the mind as so many that lived around her had done. But she could not—at least not yet. She longed for adventure—for a sunrise on a distant shore, or to walk upon a place that no one else had walked upon. But these things would never happen in the city of ash. In this city, a life of adventure was as valued as yesterday's trash. Why go out and explore the world when you could retreat into a reality of your own making? Why she was unable to retreat into the mind was never clear. In her early years, she suspected it was due to her parents' allegiance to the cult of the sea bear. But now she was not so sure. She ran her finger across a table, collecting a film of ash on her fingertips. She brought it closer to her eyes to get a good look. She suspected the ash had something to do with it. It permeated everything in the city. When people would venture outside of the cloud of ash, they would get terrible headaches. Even worse, they would find their self-made reality retreating into the deep fog of the mind. People rarely ventured outside of the city. Raven had not been outside the city either, but that was about to change. It was time to go.

She reached over the table, picked up a satchel of food, and threw it over her back. Her eyes then drifted to a shelf in the corner of the room. She looked back at the doorway and then the shelf again. Without thinking, she made her way to the shelf and began rummaging through it. It was high enough she could not see its contents. But she knew what lay there. Her fingers rolled over the hard, cold metal of a bracelet. She grasped it and brought it down. It was an ankle bracelet passed down through many generations. She blew the ash off, revealing a pyramid and a black cube. The meanings of those symbols had been lost in time. She nodded to herself as she clasped it on her ankle. As she walked out the door, she grabbed an old broom handle to use as a walking stick and took off for the far end of town. She walked with a quick pace down the street. She could not help but notice people crossing to the other side to avoid her. It had been this way since her father had died. When her mother died the prior month, the distance they kept from her doubled. It used to bother her, but now she barely noticed it.

She ran her finger along the wall of a small shop where she used to buy supplies for the models she built as a child. The trail that her finger left in the ash revealed the unkempt stone that filled the city. The wall was dark with a mold that grew there. She found it symbolic of the city, which was painted white with the ash, but underneath laid something darker—a darkness of the mind. Another person passed across the street. With the ash falling, it almost seemed like a dream. She quickened her pace. It was time to get out.

At the edge of the city, where the ash cloud tapered off, she saw an old temple that had been overtaken by the jungle. It lay just outside the cloud and thus was not usable for most. She had heard stories of children disappearing into the temple, never to be found again. She took another step. She looked back at the temple. There was something about it that pulled at her. She looked up to the sky. The sun was still early in its journey. There was time for a moment of exploration.

Up close, the extent of the jungle's claim on the building became clearer. Vines coursed around and through the old windows as if desperate to claim the building as their own. The main entrance to the temple was impassible because of a massive tree that had grown through the steps at the entrance. Looking around the side, she saw what looked like a narrow path through the mesh of vines. Without thinking, she followed it along to the back of the temple, where a crack in the rock allowed passage into the building. It was just wide enough for her to squeeze by.

Once inside, she was blinded by darkness. When her eyes adjusted, she could make out the shadows of small makeshift beds. In the middle of them were the remains of a small fire. Holding her hand just over the ashes, she still felt warmth. To her right was a set of steps that led up to the sun. She slowly made her way toward the light. At the top she found a white floor that shone bright in the rays that peeked through the holes in the roof. On the sides of the walls, she could see where vines had been scraped off in an effort to clean the room. Some were too heavily bound to the rock to remove, but it was clear that enormous effort had been taken to clear a way to the back of the temple, where a statue of a great white bear stood tall with his arms outstretched to the heavens. It was the sea bear that her parents had worshiped. She ran toward it and marveled at its size.

Her eyes followed along the girth of his legs. She wondered at how strong such a being would be if he were really here. As she followed up his belly she noticed small nicks in the stone. At first, her anger flared at the thought of someone vandalizing the bear, but as she looked closer she noticed that these were scars that had been delicately carved into the stone. The more she looked, the more she found. To have so many scars, the bear must have suffered immensely. His jawline was strong, and his fangs looked as though they were still as sharp as knives. Once she reached his eyes, she stopped and stared. Moving up the course of the bear, she had anticipated seeing rage or anger, but instead in the bear's expression she saw a deep love. She wondered at how something like that could be conveyed through carved stone.

Her eyes wandered back to the floor, where she found plaques honoring people of old. Carved into the stone at the bear's feet was the image of a woman in white holding on to the foot of the bear. Raven knelt down to get a closer look. She expected to see fear in the woman's eyes but instead found the same sense of love she had found in the bear's eyes. Her mind was lost in thought when she heard a scratch on the floor behind her. Her head whipped around to find three small children watching her.

The middle one pointed his finger at the image of the woman on the floor. "She died a long time ago serving the bear." He was a small boy covered in tattered clothes that Raven guessed was around seven years of age.

A small girl to his right, about the same age, nodded. "That's right, Jack. She was very brave. She was taken to the dragon that destroyed this island."

A boy that must have been at least ten years old, standing behind the younger children, peered into Raven's eyes as if searching for something. "She believed to the end and then was taken to the bear through fire."

Raven looked at their dirty faces and smiled. "What are your names?"

The older boy smiled back. "I'm Jason, and this is Jack and Lilly."

Raven nodded as she knelt down. They were too young to feel the mind-numbing effect of the ash. It usually took hold around thirteen years old. In the city, younger children were thought to have a mental disorder until they finally were overtaken by the ash. She was now twenty and still had not succumbed to it, but she knew it was only a matter of time. Everyone did eventually.

"My name is Raven." Raven looked back down at the lady on the floor. "How do you know so much about the lady on the floor?"

Jack pointed to the statue of the bear.

Raven looked up at the statue of the bear. "Oh! The bear told you! Is he telling you something right now?"

Lilly looked at Raven as if she were crazy. "That is a statue of the bear. It is made of stone. It cannot talk. The real bear told us." Jack and Jason nodded in agreement.

Raven nodded, not knowing what to think. "Where do you live?"

Jason pointed toward where Raven had entered the temple.

Raven looked around. "You live here? Where are the adults?"

Jack's face went gray as he turned his head away.

Jason put his hand on Jack's shoulder. "We don't talk about the adults here. It brings back bad memories. We and the other children are on our own."

Raven reached out and put a hand on Jack's other shoulder. "Sorry about making you feel sad, Jack." She then looked up at Jason. "Where are the rest of the children?"

"Some are exploring the forest that's outside of the ash. Some make it back. Others don't. Some will go back into the city. But we won't go back into the ash." Jason then put his hand on the leg of the bear. "We're with the bear."

Raven smiled at Jack, who looked as though he had not had a meal in a week. What little fat he still had did little to fill in the shallows of his eyes.

Raven opened her knapsack and laid her food out before them. "Help yourselves."

Jack and Lilly inched closer to the knapsack but stopped as Jason touched their shoulders. The two children looked up and nodded. They sat still as they quietly said something under their breath.

Raven looked down in amazement. "Aren't you hungry?"

Lilly opened one eye a little and waved her hand toward Raven. "We give thanks to the bear for all that we get, just as the bear gives thanks to the Old One."

Later, six older children made it back to the temple. Raven stayed with the children that night and dreamed of the bear.

CHAPTER 4

ON THE HUNT

THE NEXT MORNING, RAVEN woke early. She went a short way into the jungle and gathered some fruits. When she returned, the children were awake. She laid the fruits in front of them and looked at the oldest of the group. "How many are lost in the forest?"

The children held hands for a moment, and then the eldest picked up a piece of fruit and started to eat. "It's hard to know. Some go deep into the forest. Some we haven't seen for years. It's easy to get lost in the forest. The sun doesn't shine in the deep. It's easy to get turned around."

RavenTenom handed a piece of fruit to one of the smaller children. "If they know they can get lost, then why do they go?"

Jack lifted up his face with fruit running down his chin. "There's not much food here. There's not much hope either. We all came here to get out of the city ... but this isn't much of a home." Heads nodded in the room. "We've looked ... but not too far out. If you go too far in, you won't come out." Everyone nodded in agreement.

Raven sat silent for a moment and then leaned over and grabbed a piece of charcoal out of the fire pit. As she got up to head out into the forest, the oldest boy grabbed her arm.

"You will need more than a piece of charcoal if you go into the deep forest." The other children looked at him and nodded. Jason then led Raven up to the statue of the bear. Behind it was a small hidden door. The boy opened the door and pulled out a long knife the length of his arm.

"The bear told us someone would come to help us. He said that we were to give this to you."

Jason handed the knife over to her Tenom. It was in a sheath with a strap that allowed it to be worn across her back. Raven pulled the blade from the sheath and ran her finger along it. On its sides were engraved images of the bear. The pictures seemed to tell a story of some sort. She sheathed the blade and patted the boy on the back.

Raven then headed out into the forest with the three oldest children, each of whom also held a piece of charcoal. As they moved into the forest, they marked trees as they went. An hour into the forest, they ran across a wide trail littered with broken limbs. Jason knelt down and looked at the tracks. "These are from giant fire lizards." As they passed deeper into the forest, they ran across many such paths. They spent hours on the paths but found no one. Raven looked up toward the sky, but there was only the green of the canopy. They would need to return soon. As she marveled at how high the tree went, she noticed what initially looked like a vine hanging from one tree to the next. As she followed it along, she could make out a network of single-limb bridges up high.

"Let's get back to the temple before it gets dark." Raven waved the children in. She gave one last look up high. She would return here, but better prepared. They followed their marks back to the children's home and slept well that night.

CHAPTER 5

TREASURES IN THE FOREST

WHEN THE SUN ROSE, Raven gathered all the children and led them around the city to the sea. The waters were shallow for almost a mile out from the rocky shore. Coursing around the large rocks that peppered the shallow waters were thousands of silvery fish. Raven taught the children to make spears from nearby trees, and together they waded into the waters.

Raven made a game of spearing the fish, and soon they had as much as they could carry. They took the fish back to the temple and prepared them to dry. Over the next several weeks, they traveled together back and forth between the sea and the forest, collecting food. They all practiced climbing the trees and walking the great limbs up high. Some days Raven would sit up high on the limbs, watching the birds fly from branch to branch. During those times, she would gather twigs and leaves, and at night she and the younger children would create small stick birds with wings made of leaves.

One day Raven took some colored mud near the seashore and painted her face to look like one of the bright birds she watched in the forest. The children quickly followed suit. Over the next several months, they took provisions in with them and spent days to weeks in the forest, walking the high branches of the trees, looking for the lost children. During each expedition, they went farther and farther into the forest. The children carried their fish spears, and Raven her long blade. They moved together like a tribe through the forest, making sure to keep clear of the ash cloud that covered parts of the forest. It was five months into their searching when they picked up a fresh trail.

Raven pointed to a recently carved sign on a tree. Two of the smaller children nodded. Below, several giant fire lizards were uprooting tree stumps, looking for a meal. The three quietly raced along from one tree branch to another, motioning the rest of the tribe to follow. Far ahead, Raven could see a shaft of light through the canopy. She pointed toward it, and the children followed as they sped across the upper limbs. When they reached the light, they found an opening in the forest with a stream running through it. On top of the stream was an old mill with a roof that had been recently patched with wide leaves.

Raven and the children slowly slid down the trees and made their way toward the house. When they were halfway across the opening, a rock flew from the window and landed near their feet. Raven lifted up her hand, and everyone stopped. She then took the sack from her back and opened it on the grass. She laid out the dried fish and fruit and motioned the children to pull back with her to the forest edge. For a moment the forest was silent, and then, very slowly, three young boys emerged from the old mill and advanced on the food Raven had laid out. Their skin held tight to their bones as they stood over the meal before them. Just as they began to hold hands, a small girl from Raven's tribe came out from the forest and waved. The boys looked at her for a moment, and then one waved back. She slowly walked toward the boys and held one of their hands. They then closed their eyes for a moment as they gave thanks, and then they sat down and ate. When they were done eating, the boys followed the little girl to Raven.

One of the boys looked up with sunken eyes. "We've been lost for a long time. We are ready to come back."

Raven knelt down, opened her arms, and gave the little boy a hug. The others closed in on her, and they all held on to each other for some time. Raven then looked down at the boy. "Are there others here?"

"Some will come back near sunset. They are out looking for food. Many have been lost to the ash in the forest. The fire lizards find them when they lose their minds to the ash, but the ash forest is where the food is here. We are still young enough to go in."

Raven nodded. "Then we'll wait for your friends to return, and we will lead you back home."

The boy tugged on her shirt. "We've heard of a small path that leads to a place beyond the forest—a place that is safe from the monsters and the darkness. It's what each of us was looking for before we got lost."

Raven motioned the rest of the children to go into the mill, and there they lit a fire and set half of the food they carried with them out onto a table. There they waited until sunset, when seven other children arrived. They were met at the door by the three young boys. They all ate together that night, and in the morning everyone set out for home together.

CHAPTER 6

STRANGERS ON THE BEACH

SEVERAL MONTHS LATER, RAVEN was out fishing in the shallows with the children when they saw two adults walking along the shore toward the city. She tapped Jason's shoulder and pointed. He nodded.

"I have never seen any adults outside of the city. But we never used to come near the ocean. Where do you think they came from?"

Raven shook her head. "We need to watch the beachfront until we see them heading back to wherever they came from. Then we will follow them. Maybe they know the path to a better place."

Word of the plan spread quickly throughout the tribe. That night Raven and the children hid at the forest's edge.

Jack tugged at Raven's shirt and pointed at two adults carrying rolls of cloth on their back. Raven waited until they were almost out of sight to give the signal. With a touch to her nose, the forest came alive as the children followed the two from the edge of the forest.

For several hours they tracked along until they hit a high ridge of the mountain. In the full light of the moon, the two disappeared into the rock. Raven's eyes grew wide, and without thinking, she sprinted toward the point to where she had last seen them. She looked all around, feeling on the stone wall of the cliff for a passage of some sort, but she found only rock. After a great while of searching, Jack called out, "There are some tracks over here."

Raven and the rest of the children came racing over. There in the shadow of the rock, behind a crack in the mountain, was a footprint. The crack in the rock did not look as if it went anywhere, and it was barely wide enough for a person to squeeze through. Raven studied the crack for a moment, debating the safety of taking the children through it. As she stared, Jack slipped into the crack and was gone.

"Well, so much for caution!" Raven squeezed in behind the boy. Once in the crack, it was pitch black. It widened a little after the first squeeze but stayed tight. "Everyone hold hands as we go through."

Raven reached back into the face of Lilly. Lilly grabbed her hand. Together they slowly made their way up the narrow trail through the dark. After an hour they emerged from the crack on top of the ridge. Jack was waiting for them when they arrived. Raven looked at him with a stern face and then smiled and ruffled his hair. "You had enough courage for all of us, Jack."

Jack smiled and pointed to a faint path along the top of the ridge. Raven nodded and then looked back toward the city. She could see its lights through the haze of ash that hung down on it. The cloud hovered like a ghost over the forest, making its way up to the top of the mountain, where it glowed red. That mountain was the source of much strife. She thought to herself that one day she would go to the top of the mountain to see the source of the cloud for herself. Her eyes drifted back toward the path in the grass leading up the ridge. The children had already started hiking toward the horizon.

They followed the path through the night and into the next day. The narrow ridge had flattened out into a grassy plain. The youngest children reached the end of the path first. It led up the very edge of a cliff. When Raven reached them, they were standing on the edge, looking off at the channel that separated them from the next island. The cliffs were tall, and the chasm wide. Raven ran her hand through her hair. "Where did those people go? No one could cross that."

Raven looked down at the raging water below. She leaned over to see the wall of the cliff. "Even if they could climb, there is no way that a person could cross that water. They would drown or get swept out into the ocean."

There was no joy in the faces of the children. Lilly kicked a rock over the edge. "We were so close." A tear ripped loose from her eyelash in the wind. "It's worse to see it and know that we can never enter than to know that it didn't really exist."

At that moment, a bright red kite with a woman hanging underneath, steering it, shot up from deep in the chasm. She was barely within hearing range as she waved to Raven and the children and shouted, "We will be back tomorrow. We can't take you today."

With that the kite was swept away by the wind toward the far island. A blue kite joined her in the middle of the chasm. Raven watched as they glided to and fro like birds playing in the sky. It was the most beautiful thing she had ever seen. They slept on the open ground near the cliff.

CHAPTER 7

THE CALLING

That night a young man wandered through the ash city. He staggered from one building to the next, swaying as if the world itself were crumbling away. If his mind had been clear, he would have seen that the ash-covered roads were quietly sleeping, wrapped in a blanket of trash. But his mind was anything but clear. A vision of a woman and a child flashed across his eyes. How did they fit into the jumbled thoughts of his mind? His reality shimmered like a reflection on a pool in the rain. Driving his disturbed vision was the image of a great bear ripping and tearing at what he thought was real. Claws ripped through memories and dreamed visions. The vision of his life that he had held tightly to only a week ago now lay in shreds in the corners of his mind. Even in his waking eye he saw the bear. He looked down at his hand and saw a hammer; on his belt swung several chisels. Was he a craftsman of some sort? He searched his mind, but no answers came. Everywhere the white ash fell. He breathed it in, and his vision briefly cleared … but as soon as his grasp on reality firmed, it was shattered by the unrelenting clawing of the bear. Redd reached out with his hands, trying to stop the claws in his mind, but they found only ash.

Redd had passed through the center of the city, where the ash was the heaviest. He was now near the very edge of the cloud. The ash was thin here—not strong enough to overtake his mind, but strong enough to cloud his thoughts. The vision of the bear was now vivid in his mind's eye. The eyes of the bear bore down on him and through him. He wrapped his arms around his chest. He felt naked—exposed. There was a small shop near the very edge of the cloud. He dared not go any further. There he cut a deal with the owner to work for room and board. He needed time to think, to settle his mind. But always in the shadows of his thoughts was the bear. That night there was no quiet sleep. That night his mind wrestled with the bear.

CHAPTER 8

NEW FLYING FRIENDS

THE NEXT MORNING, RAVEN and the children sat on the edge of the cliff with their legs hanging over. They had awakened at the break of dawn and had been staring across the chasm for several hours now.

"There ... near the clump of dark trees." Jason pointed at a flash of red and blue on the opposing cliff's edge. They were only faint dots from the distance.

They all held their breath as the dots jumped from the cliffs and fell toward the roaring water below. Lilly put her hands on her eyes. "They will never make it."

Oohs and aahs followed as the kites with their pilots pulled out of their drop and soared high into the emptiness that lay in front of them. Time seemed to stand still as they flew across the chasm and landed lightly on the ground just behind the children.

A young woman took off a leather helmet that was strapped under her chin, turned, and looked at the children with her hands on her hips. "What do we have here?"

Her fellow pilot turned and, after looking at the children, broke out into a belly laugh. "So this is the invasion from the city that we have so long feared."

Raven stood and held out her hands. "We are not here to invade anything. We only want a better place away from the cloud of ash."

The woman smiled, looked over to the man, and then looked back at Raven. "We have found city dwellers wandering in the forest. Many have a hard time adjusting out of the ash. We have returned them all. They could not adjust to the reality that is."

Raven approached the woman. "Our minds have not yet been taken by the ash. They are too young, and I am odd. We will not miss the ash, and we cannot go back."

The woman looked at the man, and both nodded. She then turned back toward Raven and hugged her. "My name is Liney, and this is Tracker. We live on the island across the way. We are the only ones. There are three other islands farther on. We have been on all but the last. We will carry you across the way, but we must wait until the evening, when the winds change back. With the smaller children, we may be able to carry two a piece; the others we will carry one at a time."

Raven smiled. "I am Raven, and these children are my tribe." The children all smiled. "We will fly with you to your island. You will take me last, after everyone has made it over."

CHAPTER 9

MYSTERY AT THE CLOUD'S EDGE

A WEEK LATER, REDD found himself working on a stone wall near the very edge of the ash cloud. The owner of the building Redd was now living in was happy to take in a skilled craftsman that was willing to work at the edge of the city. It was the most undesirable place to live and work, according to the elite social circles. They loved the center of the city, where the ash was thick. There their minds could be totally overtaken by a reality of their choosing. It was from near the center of the city that Redd had come. He was in no hurry to return. In fact, he meant not to. In just a week's time, his mind had cleared to the point where he could slowly put together where he had been for the last several years of his life. He had left a wife and a child to his former life. He had thought of going back in for them but had thought better of it. He would never make it back into the center of the city without losing his mind. Even if he could, he would never be able to convince them to live on the periphery, as he did now. It would seem madness to them.

Redd looked at the road outside of the ash. It was strange to see dirt and trees without a thin coat of white over them. They seemed so bright. It was beautiful but at the same time seemed odd. His whole life had been dulled by the ash. To see the world without the ash was frightening. He had given some thought to walking down the road and leaving the ash forever, but to leave the ash entirely was unthinkable. He smiled, looked down at the stone he was chipping away, and laughed. He dared not go forward or back. In a sense, he was trapped in the middle of two worlds: one where he would be lost in his own mind, and the other existing totally out of his mind. Something then caught the corner of his eye.

A small child walked by on the ash-laden road toward the edge of the cloud. Redd froze for a moment as he watched the child walk. It seemed as if he were being led, and yet he was alone. After a moment, Redd came to his senses. He dropped his tools and ran for the child to stop him before he made it to the edge of the ash, but he was a second too late. The child passed out of the edge of the cloud and onto the brown dirt. Redd stopped just inches short of the outer boundary of the cloud. The boy looked back and smiled, his hand held high as if he were holding on to something bigger than himself. Redd tried to say something, but he could not. No words would come. He lunged to reach out to the little boy to bring him back in, or have the boy pull him out—which one he did not know. He only longed to be near the boy. The child turned and walked a short way down the path to a ruin by the side of the road—an old temple of some sort. The boy disappeared around the corner, leaving Redd alone only inches from the edge of the cloud. He turned and headed back to his work. It would be madness to leave the cloud entirely.

CHAPTER 10

FREEDOM

RAVEN AWOKE ALONE ON the side of the cliff. Her food had now run out, and her stomach rumbled. She looked out to the sun. It was the time of the day when Liney should be coming for her. Like clockwork she looked across the chasm, and there she saw the bright red kite take off from the opposite cliff. Raven stood mesmerized as she watched the kite fly. It was as if she were watching freedom herself spread her wings and leave the shackles of this world.

Liney landed behind Raven and unstrapped. She pulled a sack from her back and laid out its contents on the ground. It was just a few pieces of fruit and some dried fish, but it looked like a feast to Raven. Raven looked up at Liney. "How did you learn to fly?"

Liney took a bite of mango. "Tracker taught me, and his father taught him. Tracker builds the kites now. You caught us going into the city to get fabric for new kites."

Raven nodded. "Why didn't you lose your mind in the ash? The market is close to the center of the city."

"We chew on the leaves of the uba tree before entering the cloud of ash. It protects the mind for a few hours." Liney then pointed at her forehead. "But it does not protect from the headache to follow. We go as little as we can."

"The children speak of paradise beyond the forest of ash." Raven took a bite of fish.

Liney shook her head. "There is no perfect place … but we love it. There is enough food for us to live on, and it is the best island to fly from. The third island has more fruit trees and good fishing near its beach, but the winds there are unpredictable."

Raven nodded. "There are giant fire lizards throughout the ash forest. Do you have any on your island?"

Liney took a bite of fish. "Those deranged animals are confined to the main island. They are created by the ash cloud … and perhaps something more. The animals are natural on the other islands."

Raven and Liney hiked around the upper plain of the main island for most of the rest of the day, waiting for the winds to change. When the sun hung low, they returned to the cliff.

Liney strapped herself in and then strapped Raven to her. Raven walked to the edge of the cliff and looked up toward the sky. Liney began to explain the rules as Raven jumped, pulling them all off the cliff. Liney pulled back hard on the kite. A strange mix of terror and joy swirled within Raven. She stretched her arms out wide. She was flying.

When they reached the other side, they hiked to Liney's house. There all the children were watching Tracker build a kite. They helped as they could. A large piece of meat was roasting over an open fire near the cabin. The children looked to Raven and smiled.

Tracker signaled Raven and Liney to come over. "If the children are going to be here for a while, we will need something to keep them busy."

Liney nodded.

"How about making them a puzzle to put together. You are good with your hands."

Liney looked back at the children. "That's a fascinating idea. We'll get to work on that tomorrow."

That night at the meal, the children held hands and closed their eyes. Liney and Tracker looked over to Raven, who smiled and nodded. They reached out to an open hand, and one of the eldest children gave thanks to the bear. The children slept well that night.

CHAPTER 11

A LEAP OF FAITH

THREE MONTHS LATER, RAVEN looked out at the chasm toward the main island. She was strapped tight to a green kite that Tracker had made for her. She looked over the edge and then back at Liney, who gave her a thumbs-up. She took a step off the cliff and was absorbed by the wind. She soared low toward the surface of the rumbling water below and then pulled back, catching the updraft as Liney had taught her. The kite accelerated up into the sky. It was like being dipped in freedom itself. The wind howled loudly in her ears, and she howled back in turn. If someone could be one with the wind, it was her.

She landed a little hard on the other side. She tied the kite down and waved to Liney, who waved back and disappeared from view on the other cliff. Raven strapped on her pack and moved out toward the city. The sun shone bright on her face this morning, and she felt good about her decision to go back to the temple of the bear. In a dream, she had seen children seeking refuge in the temple. She needed to bring them to safety. She had established a small village on the third island for the children, where they were finding a new rhythm in life. They would be fine for a few months while she gathered more lost children into the tribe.

Her feet were light as she followed the trail back to the beach where she had first seen Liney and Tracker coming into the city. She had walked through the night without stopping. When she arrived at the temple, there were seven children waiting for her. Their faces were dirty, but there was no concern on their faces. They told her they were expecting her.

The next morning, she took the children out to the ocean to teach them to fish. As she passed by the road, she saw a man working on a stone wall near the edge of the ash cloud. His features were slightly blurred by the ash. She smiled and waved without thinking. The man looked up for a moment but didn't move. He then waved and watched her and the children make their way down toward the ocean.

CHAPTER 12

NEW BEGINNINGS

TWO MONTHS LATER, REDD dreamed he was waist-deep in ash. He was wading through it like a man might wade through a river running against him. The level of the ash was rising fast. To his right, he could see the edge of the ash cloud. There on the dirt road stood a great bear, motioning him to cross the line. The ash was now up to his neck. He felt light-headed, as if he were close to passing out. He brought his right hand out to the very edge of the cloud and felt fur run along his fingers. Everything then went dark, and he woke up. He wiped his face with his sleeve, breathing hard. The dreams were now coming every night. He got up out of bed and poured a pitcher of cold water over his head. He did not know how much longer he could go on with these dreams. He had a quick bite to eat and headed out to work on his wall. He had moved closer and closer to the temple ruins, hoping to see the woman again. Occasionally he would see her disappear into the forest with the children; other times she would head toward the ocean. She would wave, and he would wave back. She looked so bright—so beautiful. He longed to go and meet her, but he would have to leave the cloud to do so. He knew her name was Raven. He had heard the children speak her name. They also spoke of a large green kite that she flew. He pictured himself flying high in the sky with her, escaping the ash cloud that held him so tight.

That day he could hardly work. His mind swirled with thoughts of leaving, but he had had those thoughts before. He would come to the very edge and even stretch his hand out of the cloud, but that was as far as he could ever go. It was as if the cloud gripped onto him like the hands of many generations, pulling him back to the conformity of the cloud. He could feel those hands holding him even now. Evening was now upon him. He looked down at his bed. He did not want to go to sleep and dream that dream again. He put his shirt and shoes back on and looked toward the door. How many times had he tried to just walk out of the cloud? Why would this time be any different? Those thoughts would have to wait, as his feet were already passing through the doorway toward the road.

The evening sun turned the fringe of the ash cloud shades of fiery orange and red. Redd could see that glow coming. He thought back to all the small children he had seen pass out of the cloud. They always held their hands up as if holding on to something. He raised his left hand up to the level of his shoulder. He was only a few steps away from the outer boundary of the cloud when he felt the warm fur of something very large next to him. Redd looked to his left, and there was the bear from his dreams, walking beside him. The great bear turned to look at Redd. "This is your time to leave your old life and begin a new one. Just hold on to me and keep walking."

Redd's mind churned as he tried to process the fact that the bear was next him and he was about to walk out of the cloud. "I want to leave the cloud, but I cannot. I have tried many times."

"Look around you, Redd; you are already out."

Redd clenched the fur of the bear's side. "I don't know what to do. I'm afraid."

"We will do together what you could not alone."

Redd looked over to the temple ruins to his right. Redd saw Raven outside of the cloud for the first time and she was beautiful. Tears began rolling down his eyes. He slowed his pace, but the bear pulled him along. The bear turned and looked at Raven. Redd saw their eyes meet. Redd looked back at Raven but could not let go of the bear. "It was you that led the children to the temple. Isn't that where we are going?"

The great bear picked up his pace. "That is not your path, Redd. I have work for you to do. I know that you long to be with Raven. You will see her again. But the time for that has not yet come. I am Soman. I am the one that has been with you in your dreams."

They walked down the road until they reached the ocean's edge. Redd could hear the waves break on the shore. He slowed as they neared the water, but Soman did not. The water now glowed red in the sunset. Redd held tight as he waded up to his waist in the water. They walked to the very edge of the shallows, where the ocean's floor dropped off dramatically. There they found a rowboat floating empty near the deep water. Soman looked back at Redd with a serious look on his face. "The heart must be challenged for it to grow, Redd. Climb into the boat."

Soman came close to the boat and pointed to the bow. "There you will find a golden ring tied to a rope. That is how you will come aboard the *Eros*."

Redd picked up the ring, and a strong wind began to blow, leading him out to sea. "What's the *Eros*?"

Soman stayed where he was as the boat floated away. "Hold the ring up in the air, Redd, and trust in me."

Redd turned to the sound of a ship cutting through the waves. In the distance, he saw a white bear leaping from wave to wave, coming straight at him. Redd turned back to Soman for instructions, but all he saw was open water. Redd turned back toward the charging bear but began to make out the outline of a ship that blended into the horizon of the ocean so well that it could only barely be seen. The one thing that he could see clearly was a spear twice the length of a man jutting out of the front of the boat, just behind the white bear's left foot. The spear was heading straight at him. He looked down into the boat for an oar or something he could use to flee but there was nothing but a coil of rope. Redd looked back up at the approaching ship, which was now nearly upon him. The spear seemed to be coming straight at his head. He looked up at his arm, which was holding the gold ring high. Had he been holding it there the whole time? Before he could answer his own question, the ring was snatched out of his hand by the spear. The ship then veered hard right, pushing a great wave toward the tiny rowboat. Redd looked down at the rapidly disappearing coil of rope. He followed the rope with his eyes to where it tied onto the front of the rowboat. At that moment the rope tightened like a string on a guitar. Simultaneously the wave lifted the boat high in the air. The rowboat then left the water, held tight by the rope, and landed softly on the quarterdeck of the ship. Redd froze with his hands held wide, waiting for a hard impact that was not coming.

A man about his age held out his hand to help Redd out of the boat. "Welcome to the *Eros*, Redd. We have been expecting you. My name is Tanner."

Tanner smiled and pulled Redd's hand down from his forehead. "It's the only way you can board her ... and that spear did not slice into your forehead. It only came close.

That spear is not the most dangerous thing out on the open sea, Redd." Tanner led him to a chest in the middle of the main deck. He opened it and began rummaging through an assortment of weapons. He held up an axe as if sizing it over Redd but then shook his head. He then pulled out a spear with a hook on it. He handed the spear to Redd, who weighed it in his hand. The dark wood of the shaft was smooth and cold.

Redd looked down at the spear, not sure whether he should take it or not.

At that moment, the wind picked up and filled *Eros*'s sail. She took off like a wild horse, throwing Redd back on his butt. Tanner stood over him, smiled, and laid out his battle gear. "We have but one purpose on the *Eros* ... to serve the bear by making these waters safe. Gear up, Redd. You are about to see the darker things of the sea."

CHAPTER 13

A SONG OF WAR

10 Years Later

FROM THE DISTANCE, A great white bear leaped from wave to wave in the open sea. Chasing close behind was a glimmer of green and blue whose form faded in and out like that of a ship. A strong gust of wind passed over the ship, and the sky rippled above, revealing feathery gray-blue sails that faded into the horizon. As the ship closed in, Redd could make out the hind quarters of the carved wooden bear blending into the bow of the ship. He bit down on his cigar as he waved a rope with a gold ring in the air. His feet braced hard on the floorboards of the tiny rowboat. A long black spear lay at his feet next to a bucket full of fish that sloshed back and forth as the little boat tossed about in the waves. His crew would have slowed down to pick him up if they could, but they could not. *Eros* was a ship with sails that had a mind of their own and no rudder to steer her by. She sailed at the command of the wind and now was moving full clip at him. A spear the length of two men jutted out of the hull just behind the carved bear at the bow. Its tip bounced wildly like an angry swarm of bees as *Eros* crested a wave. It was heading straight at him. If he had to throw the ring in his hand onto that spear, he would miss a thousand times for every success. But that was not the way of *Eros*. His role was to stare her down as she shot straight at him, perfectly still, his hand held out with the ring.

Redd stood six feet tall and was built of strong stock. He leaned into the next wave. A quick breeze sprayed a salty mist across his face, blowing his long brown hair from his eyes. The white bear was almost upon him, the spear narrowing in toward the point between his eyes. Redd held his ground and let out a great battle cry. If he was to die today, then he would leave this world loudly. But today was not his day. The spear racing across the surface of the water missed his head by inches and snared the golden ring. With a sudden shift in the wind, *Eros* veered hard to the right. A mighty wave raised the rowboat as high as *Eros*'s quarterdeck as the slack in the rope gently tightened. The moment the rope was tight, the rowboat took flight and landed on the deck of the *Eros* like a bird landing on the tip of a branch. Redd stepped out of the rowboat and onto the bright white planks of the quarterdeck with an inch of ash still on his cigar. His foot scraped across the top of one of the three dragon scales nailed onto the side of the boat. Each was the size of a full battle shield.

"Did you throw the big one back, Redd?" Tom, the youngest member of the crew, looked up with a smile and grabbed the bucket of fish from the rowboat. He stood as tall as Redd, but at thirteen had not yet filled out.

Redd smiled and tapped off his ash in the rowboat. Tom had joined the crew only a year ago. He was the youngest man he had ever seen *Eros* pick up. Redd pulled up the fishing net and offered it to Tom.

Tom laughed as he backed away with the fish. "I thought she was going to spear you for sure." Tom skipped over to the edge of the quarterdeck and swung down to the main deck with one hand on a rope, the other swinging the pail of fish. "We don't need to go looking for that one, Redd; she'll find us soon enough."

Redd looked down at the dragon scales on the side of the rowboat— the scales of a beast that could not be killed but only fought. He ran his hand over its smooth surface. The sun often played tricks as it danced in the deep blues and purples of the scales. It was said that what a man wanted most could be seen as if through a mist in those scales, but Redd held to none of that. Making his way to the side of the ship, he looked down the one-hundred-foot side rail toward the spear at the front of the boat. He remembered the first time he had boarded the *Eros* with the spear ten years back and his surprise when he found himself on the quarterdeck, still breathing. It was the only way to board the *Eros*, a ship without an anchor that was forever in motion on the sea. It was ten years to the day that he came to be in the service of the great bear—the namesake of the carved bear at the bow of the ship.

A fish smacked Redd across the face. "Daydreaming again, Redd? What was she wearing this time?" Tanner smiled as he held the fish in one hand and played with its mouth with the other as if it were blowing a kiss to Redd.

Redd grabbed him around the shoulders and pulled him in tight. "What would I do without you, Tanner?"

Tanner smiled and threw the fish back into Tom's bucket. "You would have sunk down to the bottom of the ocean without me. That be for sure."

Redd smiled and nodded as he grabbed a long pole with a hook on it. He made his way to the bow of the ship and fished the ring off of the spear and laid it back in the rowboat. He looked out at the open sea. The only interruption of the smooth line of the horizon was five small peaks sticking out of the water. It was his homeland. It seemed early to be heading back toward the island. Their provisions were only half spent. *Eros* suddenly lurched forward like a falcon who had just spotted her prey. The ship lifted high on the water as her hull sung a song of foaming sea.

The crew sang as they reached for their battle gear.

Free men are we
that sail the sea
in service of the bear.
Our hearts sing out
both bold and stout
in the love we share.
No dreams have we forgone
while serving hard and strong,
for our hearts have been remade
to love to fight the shade—
that evil that lurks deep
and through dark waters creeps.

Free men are we
that sail the sea
in service of the bear.
Our hearts sing out
both bold and stout
in the love we share.
Many friends have we lost,
their lives the final cost.
Though before each one went down
and claimed his golden crown,
joy filled their hearts intense;
the bear's love is all they sensed.
Free men are we
that sail the sea
in service of the bear.
Our hearts sing out
both bold and stout
in the love we share.
So bring us monsters while we sail
with horn and fang and purple scale.
Though we may die as those we love
while fighting evil tooth and glove,
we will die free, desires spent,
our hearts aflame, fully content.
Free men are we
that sail the sea
in service of the bear.
Our hearts sing out
both bold and stout
in the love we share.

Each of the crew donned tight-fitting leather pants that were cut off below the knee. Blades stuck out at the knee, as well as on the leather straps that covered their forearms. Their sandals were light, with one-inch spikes on the soles. Redd often thought they would make good climbing gear for the peaks of his island. He chuckled as the thought left his mind. Their use was for a much more dangerous climb.

Redd opened a large chest that was nailed down in the center of the deck and pulled out a spear hewn from a dark wood with a hook just under the head. Each of the thirteen men grabbed a weapon from the chest and ran to the side of the ship. If there was any fear left in their hearts, it did not show. Their eyes gleamed with a hunger for the adventure to come. With each passing wave, the anxieties of their past lives had passed away. Each had come to accept the way of *Eros*, for to follow *Eros* was to follow the bear. Each had made an oath out of love to the bear to protect these waters with his life. Obedience was now the rhythm of their joy.

"We be heading through the straight!" Tanner yelled as he raised a broadsword. There was a smile on his face like that of a man who has seen food for the first time in a month.

The island had been splintered into five pieces ages ago, leaving sheer cliffs five hundred feet high with only three hundred feet between them. The main island was crowned with a smoking mountain that rumbled at night. The sea washed across the five islands at a slant, creating a hard break on the west sides of the straits. When the sea was calm, the water would spray one hundred feet in the air like a raging river. A normal ship would never make it through such a gauntlet. But *Eros* was not a normal ship. The wind shifted, and she picked up speed for the middle straight.

Redd's eyes were now wide open and his knuckles white as he held fast to his spear. There was only one reason *Eros* would take them through the straight. One of the beasts must have retreated into its depths. He hoped it was the great red beast the men called Vepar. She had taken five of his men since he had joined the *Eros*. All were close friends.

His eyes drifted up toward the peaks of the cliffs. A green dot left the edge of the cliff and dove down toward the waters below. It was one of the kite riders that collected precious stones from the broken islands. As the dot fell, its shape became clearer, like that of a falcon covered in deep green cloth. He had once known someone who flew such a kite.

A giant wave caught *Eros* and drove her high up the cliff only twenty feet from the jagged wall of rock. Redd's eyes shot down at the water below, where a white-and-yellow horn stirred just above the waves. It was the forehorn of Vepar, whose massive body must have been just under the foam below. *Eros* shifted right, riding the wave down toward the monster, and as she did, the kite rider zipped by her bow. She yelled as she shot by, her voice wild; her curly brown hair fluttered madly as she chased the wind. Redd caught a glimpse of her face as she flashed by, although he knew it was her before he saw her. Only one kite pilot would dip so low in the strait. It was Raven. He had thought after ten years that he would never see her again. Racing down to the surface of the water, she banked hard, unsheathed a long knife from her back, and dragged it across the surface of the water. The blade turned from silver to red as she pulled up, kicking the tip of the white horn as she barely passed over.

The blue foam of the water below turned red as the very sea seemed to come alive. With a deafening roar, a great red beast five times the size of the *Eros* rushed out of the water and chased just behind Raven. Before he could think, Redd broke into a full sprint toward the bow of the ship. Tom followed close behind with an axe in one hand. With one leap, Redd was on the tip of the white bear's nose, and with the second leap he was airborne, spear in hand. Time had no meaning as he flew thirty feet, landing hard on the back of the red monster. The blades on his leather armor sunk deep into the beast's flesh. He felt a shiver on the beast's back as Tom landed beside him. Vepar was still rising as they climbed on her back. The white-and-yellow horn was still forty feet away.

Raven veered hard left, coming back over the beast as if playing with her. She passed just over Redd, and their eyes met for only a moment. Raven then caught the updraft and shot high into the sky. Redd picked up the pace of his climb on the great beast, which was now near the apex of its surge out of the water. Out of the corner of his eye, he thought he saw Raven wave. Was she waving at him or for him to come along? His mind debated the meaning as he sprinted up to the head of the monster. Twenty feet beyond the horn, bulging out of the sleek red skin, was the first of the beast's three yellow eyes. Its diameter was the full length of a man. Redd looked into the eye and remembered why he was there. He waved his spear in the air to let the beast fully see it before he plunged it deep into the yellow globe. Tom smiled as he raised his axe on the other side. With a nod they each struck the eye with one heavy blow. White smoke erupted from where the black wood pierced the beast. Vepar let out a great yell that shook the cliffs. In moments what was once an eye became a crater of ash.

Redd looked back with Tom at the remaining eleven of his shipmates, who were farther down on the beast's back, stabbing and hacking at its flesh. White smoke and ash blew across the red landscape of Vepar's back. In apparent agony, she arched into a giant backflip and took fully to the air. Redd soon found himself hanging from his spear as the beast towered above him. He looked down below at the rushing waters of the strait.

Redd laughed and gave one more twist to the hook at the end of the spear. With that he fell through the air with eleven other men. Below in the strait, *Eros* raced across the waters, catching each of the men in her sails as they fell—all but one, that is. Redd watched as Tanner held tight to the beast's flesh and hacked deeper into its chest. As Vepar crashed down into the water, a massive wave rushed forward, lifting *Eros* halfway up the cliffs before she made it to the end of the strait and shot out of the gap like a cannonball into the open sea.

Redd looked back at the island as it grew smaller on the horizon. Tears filled his eyes as his mind filled with the image of Tanner hacking away as the beast hit the water. Now they were only twelve, and *Eros* would soon look for another, for she needed thirteen—no more, no less. The island was now just a blur through his tears. He wondered if he would see Raven again.

CHAPTER 14

A WOUNDED HEEL

RAVEN CAME OVER THE cliff's edge with just enough wind to get her over the top. As she landed, her right leg buckled and she rolled off the kite. She jumped up, waving the long knife drenched in blood as she yelled to the sky. She had made it. She turned to Tracker, who had been waiting for her.

"I saw everything, including that gash on your heel from kicking her." Tracker was smiling as he always did. He pulled out a skin of water and motioned Raven to sit down and give him her foot.

"I think I saw him!" Raven winced as Tracker cleaned the wound. "I think that was the man from the shop—the one repairing the wall in the ash near the temple. He was on that ship." Her arm motioned down to the water below.

"Come on, Raven … no ship could survive through the strait." Tracker looked down at the wound. "Maybe you were hallucinating. Sometimes there is poison on the horns of these beasts." He looked down at her foot. "I'm going to need to suck out the poison." Tracker was no longer smiling. It had been a while since those feet had been washed.

Tracker smiled and pulled the knife from his belt. He motioned for Raven's foot. Tracker looked closely at the wound, pushing his finger around it. He used his knife to cut the wound a little deeper. He then turned the knife sideways and pressed down, pushing out blood and a small piece of the horn that had been imbedded in her foot.

He handed the piece of the horn over to her, smiling. Tracker then untied a small pouch containing a needle and thread and began to sew up the wound.

49

"I saw the white bear down there."

Tracker leaned in. "What was he like?"

"He was a wooden statue nailed onto the front of a ship."

Tracker stepped back. "Preposterous. It's the white bear that keeps us safe from those things." Tracker pointed back down into the strait.

"Well, I know one thing. I saw that man on the deck of a ship down there with a white bear carved into its bow, and no one is going to convince me otherwise." Raven shook her knife toward Tracker.

Tracker looked over at the kite. The right wing was broken. "Come on; let's get you back home. I'll carry the kite. Did you find anything good on the third island?"

Raven pulled a leather bag from her side and opened the top. "Just five of the prettiest glow rocks you have ever seen."

Tracker looked in and saw five stones that had a dim green glow. "We'll be able to trade those for some more kite material. I have three that are nearly done right now." Tracker weighed the stones in his hands. "I didn't think the third island had anything left."

"It doesn't. I found a spot on the fifth island that has never been touched." Raven looked away as she spoke, knowing what was to come.

"Raven! There is a reason why we don't fly to the fifth island." Tracker stood up, his face beet red. "The drafts are unpredictable coming back. You could have been stranded there for a year ... or worse." As the red drained from his face he sat back down. "So where on the island did you find them?"

Raven smiled. "There's a cave on the far west end near the shore. At low tide you can go pretty far in. The whole thing is lit up with these stones ... and I'm pretty sure I could make out some carved stairs."

"Stairs?" Tracker rubbed his chin. "No one from the city could have gone there. If there are stairs, they must have been hewn before the island split."

"What do you mean, 'if there are stairs'? If I said I saw stairs, I saw stairs." Raven limped to her feet and grabbed her broken kite. "Saddle up, flyboy, and we'll go back and find them together."

Tracker stood and stared at Raven's broken kite and lame leg and then began to laugh. "So you saw your mystery man on a boat in the strait."

"He wasn't just on the ship ... I saw him jump onto the back of that monster, climb up its back, and stab it in the eye."

"Is that right?" Tracker's laugh was almost infectious, bringing a smile back to Raven's face.

Raven looked down at her kite, fidgeting with the broken wing. "Why do you think he left? I had always thought that if he could escape the ash, he would stay with me and the children."

"He followed the bear just like you." Tracker picked up the kite and hefted it up over his shoulder. "You saw him led out yourself. I remember you telling me the bear told you something in his eyes ... but you never said what that was." Tracker motioned Raven to follow as they started their way back to Tracker and Liney's house on the second island. "Some say he waded out into the deep water and never came back."

"Hmphh ... you know how the people of the city think about the deep water—or anything deep, for that matter. They've all gone half-crazy from inhaling the ash." Raven picked up her pace to keep up. She looked down at Tracker's boots. "Instead of kite supplies, you should think about getting some new boots."

Tracker looked down at his boots, which were more patch than leather. "We wear old boots so we can fly old kites. Let's get on home before Liney starts worrying about us."

They followed a trail that led up higher onto the mountain. Two hours later, they came upon a house built at the edge of the forest. It was not difficult to find, as it was the only house on the second island. As they came into the cabin, they saw Liney carving away at a small piece of wood. She set it down into a groove that only it would fit into. She would paint it later. Tracker looked down with Raven at the newly carved puzzle.

"Mix it up. We can do it tonight." Raven moved her hand toward the puzzle and mixed the pieces up.

Tracker looked over to Raven as he sat down. "So what did the great bear tell you with his eyes ten years ago?"

Raven lifted up a piece, studying its shape. "He said that man and I would be together someday."

CHAPTER 15

HEARTBURN

LATER THAT NIGHT, VEPAR found her way to the underground river in the volcano from which she was made. Her mighty horn scraped to a halt on the golden banks of the river. Xaphan spread his wings in shock as he bounded over to his dying creation. The great red creature then shook hard three times and rolled over. A hole in her chest shook for a moment. Xaphan leaned down to look at the wound just as the beast's heart flew out of its chest. Xaphan held his breath as he saw the heart tumble toward his treasure pile. Still watching the hole in the beast's chest, Xaphan then saw a man crawl out of the hole, holding his sword high.

The dragon roared in anger and blew flame toward the golden ceiling above. "Who is it that would dare to kill one of my creations?"

Tanner looked up at Xaphan, his body covered in blood. "I am Tanner from the *Eros*, and I will not rest until you and your abominations are dead and rotting on the floor of the sea."

Xaphan lowered his head to the level of Tanner to look him in the eye. "I will cut you into pieces and use you for spare parts, as I have done with the rest of your traitorous race." Xaphan then moved in very close to Tanner. "And I will make sure you feel every bit of it."

As soon as Xaphan was within striking distance, Tanner slashed his sword across the dragon's nostrils. Xaphan leaped back, holding his nose as Tanner ran into a nearby crack in the cave. Xaphan, regaining his senses, bounded over to the crack, and blew a stream of fire into its opening. The fire rolled through the wandering crack in the mountain and made a full loop, blowing its wrath onto Xaphan's wounded nostril. The dragon again howled in agony. Xaphan then pulled his ear close to the crack and listened closely. Within the mountain he could still hear the heartbeat of the man.

"How long do you think you can hide in that crack, little man? No food … no water … you will come crawling out on your hands and knees, and I will be waiting." Xaphan rubbed his nostril feeling the pain of the sword and the fire.

* * * * *

Tanner had backed into a side passage just before a river of fire burst through the passage he had been in. Although he could see nothing, he sensed another close by. He raised his sword and swung it here and there. "I am Tanner of the *Eros*, and I am not afraid."

"I see you, Tanner," said a voice in the dark. "You have fought well for years in my service. I have a new role for you now."

Tanner followed the voice in the dark until he found the light of day at the end of the passageway. Behind him stood a tall stone wall, in front of him a small mill in a clearing in a forest.

CHAPTER 16

A SHORT DETOUR

THE NEXT DAY, TRACKER, Liney, and Raven set off for the city to trade the glow stones. They now stood at the edge of the cliff separating them from the main island three hundred feet across the strait. Tracker and Liney looked over at Raven, who was leaning a bit to one side.

"Are you sure you want to make the flight today, Raven?" Liney looked down at Raven's right foot, which was lifted half off the ground.

Without hesitation, Raven pushed off the edge and was airborne. "There will be plenty of time to wait when we're dead."

Raven banked hard left and then right as she dove deeper into the strait as only she would. The three kites danced about in the sky like birds at play. It was far too short of a time to be in the air for Raven, but they could stretch it out only so far and still make the other side. The three adventurers landed simultaneously on the opposite cliff as though stepping off a cloud.

Raven looked up at the peak of the smoking mountain and then down at the trail that led to the city. "I wonder what makes that mountain smoke?"

Tracker nodded and looked into their provision bag as if he were calculating the dimensions of a kite wing. "I think the food would last through a little detour."

Liney nodded and took off toward the mountain. "What are we waiting for?"

Raven looked back at the kites, which they had tied down by the cliff. There was no need to hide them. No one else traveled in these parts. The people of the city held to the shallows in the east and never ventured out too far.

CHAPTER 17

A MORNING CHAT

REDD AND TOM SAT with their feet hanging over the stern of the *Eros*, watching the sun slowly creep out of the sea.

"Was it worth it, Redd? Ten years of your life fighting these monsters?" Tom threw a fish head out into a school of sharks trailing *Eros*'s wake.

"To let go of all your worries and live each moment of life as if it may be your last?" Redd pulled a piece of wood out of his pocket and began to carve on it. "It's freedom, Tom."

Tom looked over at him with a question on his face as he grabbed another fish head.

"It's freedom from an illusion. Do you remember what it was like living in the city before *Eros* took you on? Everyone owned by their own delusions? They were not free to be themselves. They are slaves to a pretend self that they spend all day propping up. They think they control their destiny. They make plans with the illusion that they are in control of their lives. It's why they won't venture into the deep waters of their own minds. There's a piece of them that knows that the whole thing is a sham and that if they look too deep, their whole pretend world will crumble around them."

"I knew someone that was different." Tom threw another fish head out, and a hammerhead shot out of the water, catching it in midair.

"Raven?"

"After my parents died, I was taken out of the city by the bear. She took me in."

Redd nodded. "She took a lot of kids in—kids that didn't fit in. She is a good woman."

Redd carved deep into the piece of wood with his knife. "It was the great bear himself that pulled me out of the city and led me here."

Redd held out the wooden figure of a woman half carved out of the piece of wood. It looked as if it were painted a deep purple from the sunrise reflecting from the water below.

"Raven would take us all out to the cliffs, and she taught us all to fly the kites." Tom looked out at the ocean. "Some of the children she would leave on the third island. It is a beautiful place. More and more would stay each trip. I think she was moving them all to the island. There were only three left when the great bear pushed me out to sea in the rowboat."

"Did Raven know you were leaving?"

He shook his head and said, "He came at night when all were asleep. He told me he had a job for me to do." Tom looked back into the bucket. One fish head left.

Redd and Tom felt a jerk as the wind pulled hard on *Eros*'s sails. The water churned behind her as the school of sharks circled in the eddies of the ship.

Redd pulled himself up with a smile. "Looks like *Eros* is on the hunt."

Tom looked over to Redd with a smile. "I think I could learn to like this."

Redd slapped Tom on his back. "What more could a man want, Tom? Service out of love of the bear. Life is just one grand adventure. You just have to let it all go." Redd rolled the wood carving in his pocket without thinking about it. "Time to suit up, Tom."

CHAPTER 18

PET SHOPPING

RAVEN WIPED THE SWEAT off her brow. There was a reason no one climbed the smoking mountain. It was steep. She looked ahead at Tracker squeezing by a boulder. "Better lose some weight if you want to make it past that boulder on the way down."

Tracker looked back, laughed, and rubbed his belly. "Remember when we got caught up here in a lightning storm?"

Liney squeezed past the boulder. "That was not a good place to be. I can still feel the tingling in my feet."

Raven nodded. "We could have all been killed." Her mind filled with the vision of a lightning bolt hitting a slab of flat rock above the tree line. She thought it would go deep into the ground at the point of impact, but that is precisely what it does not do. It scatters out on the surface of the wet rock for as far as you can see before it hits you. Raven looked up at the sky. *Baby blue, no clouds. Good.*

The hiking took place within a dense part of the forest. There was no path, as no one bothered to venture this high on the mountain anymore, and no one ever hiked the forest within the ash cloud.

Liney stopped ten yards ahead and held her arm up. She began to slowly back away as she pointed to a large thicket to the right. The thicket shook for a moment, and then a yellow lizard the size of Liney jumped onto their path. His eyes were dark blue, and on the top of his head was a small yellow horn. Liney backed past Raven, who held her ground as she pulled out her knife.

"Can't outrun a fire lizard." Raven waved her knife in the air, catching the glint of the sun on its tip.

The lizard blew a stream of fire at the thicket, reducing it to ash. It then looked up at Raven and began to bob its head to the rhythm of the motion of her knife.

"You're not going to be able to tame this one, Raven." Tracker pulled out his own knife. "It's way too big."

Raven slowly walked toward the lizard as she kept the glint of the sun on the tip of her knife. "He's still all yellow. He's just a baby."

Liney now started walking toward the yellow beast with knife in hand. "I'd hate to meet its mother."

Raven nodded, now only feet away. The beast blinked, shook its head, and a snort of smoke rose from its nose. Making sure to keep the glint on her knife, she reached around the lizard's jaw and rubbed him back and forth. "They like it right here." The beast tilted his head, wagging his tail back and forth, stirring up a dust cloud behind him.

"You've got to get them early." Raven looked back and smiled. "The older red ones are nothing but fire and fury packed into two thousand pounds of lightning-fast muscle."

Liney looked the lizard over from top to bottom. "This one's mother must have weighed about that. How do you think he got so big?"

Raven looked up at the smoking top of the mountain. "They say that the ash can have an effect on the animals too."

"So what are you going to name him, Raven?" Liney smiled, putting her knife away.

"He looks like a Charlie." Raven sheathed her knife and rubbed the beast on both sides. Charlie rolled onto his side, clearly looking for a tummy rub.

Tracker looked him over. "He could come in handy."

Raven started walking up the mountain with Charlie close behind. "Fight what, Tracker? There's nothing up there but rock and smoke."

CHAPTER 19

CHAINS

DEEP WITHIN THE VOLCANO, Xaphan slowly ran his claw across a crack in his palace. "I can hear your heartbeat in there, Tanner. How have you stayed alive for so long in your little rock prison? Did you find a passageway to the surface?" Xaphan rubbed his nose and winced. "We did not get off to a very good start. I am Xaphan. I was considered a god by your ancestors. I have known your kind since the beginning. Tell me, little man, why is it that you choose to be a slave to the bear? Does your freedom mean nothing to you?"

A voice then rang out from the rock. "True freedom can be found only in the service of the bear."

Xaphan howled with laughter. "How can you believe such a simple lie, Tanner? How many years of your short life did you spend on that lonely boat killing my creations? Think of all the pleasures of life you lost out on. And what did you get in return? The favor of the bear? Not all chains are made of iron, Tanner."

"I lived the life you speak of before the bear showed me the truth and saved me from the illusion of the ash. It was nothing compared to the love of the bear."

Xaphan's eyes glowed red. "*Love ... of ... the ... bear?!* Oh, how little you understand the workings of this world. Love is nothing but a chain that binds you into never-ending slavery. Love is an illusion ... a prison of the mind. It is the source of all pain and the driver of all sorrow. Let it go, Tanner, and follow me as your ancestors did. Follow me and be free."

"I have returned to haunt the shadows of your mountain so that you will sleep with one eye open knowing my blade is only moments away from piercing your heart."

Xaphan could hear the sound of a sword being sharpened on a rock. That grating sound continued through the night. He kept one eye on the crack in the wall that night but saw nothing other than the dancing shadows from the torches in his palace.

CHAPTER 20

LEVEY

REDD LOOKED OUT AT the horizon, hoping upon hope to see islands appear and disappear in the distance. He had a score to settle with one monster in particular, and he could feel that his time was running out. He looked over at the rowboat with the dragon scales nailed to its side. He had hoped that might provoke a confrontation with their former owner, but his little excursions had led only to a few extra fish on the menu.

"Land ho." Tom pointed off the starboard bow at a hill that appeared to be the size of the big island, which then slowly sunk back into the sea.

Redd raced back to the weapons chest on deck and pulled out his spear. The rest of the men were strapping on their battle leather like small children putting their shoes on after a nap. Each strap was meticulously tested with a tug. Equipment failure usually proved to be fatal. Several other islands popped up in the distance and disappeared.

"It's Levey for sure, Redd." One of his men pointed an axe out toward the dark waters. "Looks like you're going to get that fight you've been itching for."

Levey is what the men called her, but Redd knew her full name—Leviathan She was an immortal beast that was as old as this world. Redd braced himself for the wave that was sure to come. He looked over to Tom. This would be his first sortie with Levey. There were no words that could prepare one for it. The less one knew on the first meeting, the better.

As if on cue, the sea suddenly churned as if the foundations of the earth itself had given way. Without warning, a dragon head five times the size of *Eros* herself rocketed out of the dark froth followed by a never-ending neck covered in dark purple scales like those nailed onto the rowboat. The white deck panels shook as it let forth a great roar. They shook their weapons at the sky and all let forth a mighty battle cry. The water settled for a moment and then churned once more as the head of the dragon dove down from the clouds like a hammer toward the *Eros*. Levey's head was fearsome, with five horns in a row rolling down to her neck. She opened her mouth as she descended and took a deep breath. Redd had seen her teeth before; they were three times the size of a man. She exhaled, and he could feel a wave of heat preceding what he knew was to come. He looked over at Tom and smiled. The boy stood his ground. *Good.*

Fire erupted from her mouth, turning the blue sky red with flame. The white deck panels glowed as they reflected the blaze above. Still the men held their ground. Moments before the mammoth fireball would have engulfed the *Eros*, a great wind filled her sails and she took off like a dart. Levey's head plummeted into the water where the *Eros* had been, creating a wave fifty feet high. *Eros* rode the swell up to the crest and cut hard across the spine of the wave, riding its peak.

Redd looked down at his feet. He did not wear the spiked war sandals that they normally wore. The spikes would not penetrate those scales. He had learned that the hard way. Instead he had inset the black wood of an old weapon into the soles of each of the men's new sandals. This time it would be different.

"There she is!" Tom yelled, looking down at a rising mound of purple scales the size of the main island.

All the men jumped onto the behemoth's back. The dark wood on the soles of their sandals burned into the scales, finding strong purchase on the beast's back. The men at once began hacking away at the scales, and wisps of white smoke soon filled the air as the black wood of the weapons made contact with Levey. But Redd stood still, looking about him, waiting. And then he saw it: the island of scale tipped up ever so slightly, and the sea began to rumble off in that direction. It was what he had been waiting for. He sprinted in that direction.

Tom followed close behind. With little warning, Levey's mighty head pierced the water's surface and let out a bloodcurdling yowl.

Redd did not miss a step as he picked up his pace toward the massive neck that was now emerging out of the water. Behind him he left smoldering footprints on the beast's back. As he neared the edge of the back, he plunged his spear in and vaulted himself high in the air, landing on the rising neck. Tom followed, jumping the span and just making it to the rising neck twenty feet below Redd. They both climbed as fast as they could, but the neck was long. Redd looked up the towering neck. He would never make the climb in time. He then stopped and pulled back his spear and, with all his might, drove it deep into the beast's neck. The neck shivered, closely followed by an agonizing howl from above. Tom followed suit, and soon Redd could see Levey's head coming straight for them. Redd knew she could fry them with her breath, as her scales were impervious to flame. But that was not her way. She would try to impale them with her horns. The timing would be tight. He looked down at Tom and hoped he was up for this.

The descent of Levey's head was now nothing but a blur. She turned her upper neck, exposing the massive horns on her crown, which no man had ever touched and lived. Levey would expect them to shimmy to the back of her neck, and it was there that she would impale them both with a quick backward slash of her head. But that was not Redd's plan. He motioned Tom to be ready to jump into the horns. Then they both were airborne, high above the water. They landed hard between the second and third horns of the beast. Redd climbed fast, intent on blinding the beast that could not be killed. He and Tom soon reached the crown of her head and raced toward their prize. It was then that the ground below them gave way as Levey dropped her head and arched up, opening her jaw wide. Now in free fall, Redd looked down at the massive fangs. Tom flew by him as he grabbed the boy with one arm. With the other, he dragged the hook of his spear across the nose of the beast, leaving a smoking gash across its nostrils. Its great yellow eyes burned with hatred as they passed out of sight. Redd's arch shortened slightly when the spear released from the nostril, veering him toward Levey's front upper fang. He thrust his spear into the white wall of the tooth and flung himself and Tom clear of the lower jaw and into the free air below.

Redd looked down at the *Eros* below. Nine men stood tall. He felt the soft impact as *Eros*'s sails broke his fall. Leviathan howled as the wind drove into *Eros*'s sails and sped her away. The beast gave chase for miles but was no match for the ship's speed. The men shook their weapons at her, wanting another pass, but *Eros*, it seemed, had other plans for them. Redd surveyed the deck. They had lost yet another man to the beast. To his left, a purple scale was lying on the deck, still smoking from where it had been pried off the beast. He took a hammer and two black wooden pegs and hammered it on the side of the rowboat that rested on the quarterdeck. With his spear, he carved the fallen man's name on the bottom of the scale. He had so wanted to blind that monster, but he would have to settle for a tooth today. Later the men confirmed that the tooth he had speared had turned entirely to ash. Redd smiled at the thought of the beast without a front tooth.

That night Redd could not sleep. He went up to the quarterdeck and saw a shadow move near the stern. Redd followed, and in the dark of the night he saw the great bear staring back at him. Fear and love swamped Redd as he ran toward the bear and fell into its mighty arms. Redd did not know what to say; he could only sob as the bear held him tight.

"It has been a long time since our walk into the ocean, Redd. I have something new for you. There is one of mine that needs you more than the *Eros*. She will be at the western cliff in four days." With that the great bear tossed Redd into the sea as *Eros* brought them close to the main island. Redd came up to the surface just in time to see *Eros* blend into the horizon. He looked over his shoulder and could see the lights of the city on the main island. He was only fifty yards from the shallows. He swam until his feet could reach the sandy floor below. At least it was nighttime and he might go unnoticed by the city dwellers.

CHAPTER 21

A CLAW IN THE DARK

RAVEN AWAKENED WHEN TRACKER nudged her at sunrise. They had camped just above the tree line. The air was crisp and dry. Far above the tree line stood the rim of the mountain. Unlike the remaining four islands, whose tops were green, this land seemed cursed with only rock and dead brush. Smoke drifted from the mountain to the east. Charlie was waiting at Raven's side as she slept with a fierce look in his eyes.

"It looks like a long way up; we had better get going." Liney tightened the straps on her gear and took off.

It was a half day's hike to the steep rocks that guarded the last hundred yards of the ascent. They reminded Raven of fangs of one of the sea beasts. Jutting up into the air, they seemed angry with the sky, perhaps for some ancient slight never forgiven.

It was midday by the time they reached the rock wall. It was taller up close. Liney threw a rope with a hook on it up high onto the cliff. There were many areas of rock jutting out, and the hook caught tight on one a third of the way up. Liney pulled hard, and the rope held. She motioned the other two to follow as she started making her way up the rock.

Raven looked over to Tracker. "That looks about as safe as diving into the strait for a quick swim."

Tracker laughed. "This coming from a woman that tamed a twelve-foot fire lizard with just a knife. Maybe you should define 'safe' for me."

Raven shook her head and looked over at Charlie. "You can't follow me here, baby." Raven gave him a good rub behind the jaw. "We'll catch you on the way back." With that said, she grabbed onto the rope and gave it a tug. Liney had made it up to a ledge near where the hook had held. "Well, we didn't come up here for nothing." With that Raven began climbing the wall.

Once the three had made it up to the ledge, they looked up the remainder of the cliff.

"It looks too smooth up high to catch the hook." Liney leaned over, studying each crack. It would take days to shimmy up the narrow crevices.

Tracker pointed to the right edge of the ledge. "I think this ledge spirals up the side of the cliff."

Raven looked over to Liney. "That will take us around the east side of the mountain."

"In the smoke and ash." Liney cringed and looked back up at the cracks just above.

"If we make good time, we will only be in it for a little while." Tracker was already sliding to the right, looking around the corner. "In twenty feet it gets wide enough we could walk on it."

Liney nodded and swung around Tracker, disappearing around the corner.

It was an hour before Raven noticed the first trace of ash on her shoulder. She brushed it off like an unwanted bug. The path ahead looked like a snowstorm. "That's a lot of ash."

Tracker nodded. "Maybe we should tie up to each other in case one of us gets disoriented."

Liney was already forming loops in the rope. Raven tied a piece of cloth over her mouth to breathe through, and the others followed suit.

Liney was the first to enter the cloud of ash. Tracker lunged forward as the rope pulled him down the path. Raven took up the rear.

The first hour of walking in the ash went better than Raven could have hoped. Her mind swam with memories of the children she had brought to the middle isle. They had been doing so well that she had taken to going on long holidays with Tracker and Liney. The children had taken to the kite riding like fish to water. Raven's mind filled with the feeling of flying. She had often dreamed of flying like a bird. There was nothing more perfect than flying. With that thought, she braced in her takeoff pose and promptly dove off the side of the cliff.

Raven was the first to wake up. Liney and Tracker lay all scratched up and covered with dust in a widened area of the path. Raven jumped to her feet and shook Tracker, who moaned as he awoke. She looked left and right. Her last memory was of jumping from the cliff. Why would she have done something like that? She then looked back at the ash and remembered why. "We are not going back through that." Raven shook her fist at the cloud.

Tracker ran his hand over the surface of the cliff behind him. "This has been carved out." He looked forward down the path. "This whole path has been carved out of the mountain."

Raven slipped the rope from her waist and pulled out the long knife from the sheath on her back. "I've never heard of anyone being up here."

Liney's eyes grew wide. "Something pulled us out of the ash. She showed them her arm, which was forming a bruise in the shape of a giant claw.

Raven motioned her companions forward. "It doesn't look like we have much choice."

The next hour of the climb was steep but smooth, leading up to the edge of the mountain.

Tracker was the first to look over. A deep pit lay below, filled with an ashy smoke that glowed a dull orange. "It goes on forever. I think the glow is below the shoreline of the island."

Raven leaned over and looked down. A brisk wind blew at her back. Liney grabbed her shirt to keep her from falling in. Raven watched as the wind swirled down the mountain's center, clearing the cloud of ash and smoke to the side for only a moment. Deep in the bottom of the pit stood a giant black tree. Every limb and branch glowed with fire. As quick as the wind blew a hole in the cloud of ash, it filled back in. "Did you see that? There is a gigantic tree on fire down there. That's where all the ash and smoke are coming from."

Tracker gave Raven a funny look. "The mountain has always smoked, Raven. How could it be a tree? It would have burned up long ago."

Raven was silent for a moment, deep in thought. "There were no branches missing, and yet it was in full blaze. Even the tips of the branches seemed to be intact. It was on fire, but it wasn't burning up."

Tracker laughed. "Right. Maybe you're still a little foggy from the ash storm we just walked through."

Liney gave Tracker a stern look. "If Raven said she saw a burning tree, then that's what she saw."

They spent another three hours waiting for another view of the bottom, but the wind did not blow, and all they saw was glowing ash.

Liney looked to the west. The sun was hanging too low to wait any longer. "We need to make our way down. We can't stay up here overnight."

Raven followed the path back down. "We can't go back through the ash. I've had enough flying for one day." She looked down the path that led back into the ash and rubbed her arm. The scratches had stopped bleeding, but she would feel the brunt of the abrasions in the mornings. She looked in the other direction and saw a narrow switchback continuing around the crater. "I think this narrow path is our best bet."

The switchback went on for several miles and eventually led to a set of stairs cut into the rock of the mountain.

Tracker looked down the long flight of stairs leading to the tree line far below. "How could we not know that this was here?"

Liney began the climb down. "Why would we know? We have no reason to come up this side of the mountain, and the villagers live in the ash cloud. Any stories of this crater would have been forgotten long ago."

They reached the tree line just before dusk. Liney looked down at the claw mark on her arm. "Maybe we should keep going." She pointed at a path that continued down the mountain into the forest.

Tracker started putting up their shelter. "The forest isn't safe at night, and we don't know that path. For better or worse, we are stuck here for the night."

CHAPTER 22

THE MARKET

THAT NEXT MORNING, THE three broke camp and headed down the path into the forest.

"This path looks like it's been used pretty frequently." Tracker ducked under a branch. "But I don't recognize any of the tracks."

"There is something wrong with a tree that burns forever, creating a perpetual cloud of toxic ash. I think we need to do something about that." Raven jumped over a couple rocks that had rolled onto the path.

"What are you going to do Raven? There's no way down there. It would take a lifetime to make a rope long enough to climb down. And even if you could get down without being suffocated by ash and smoke, what would you do?" Tracker stubbed his toe on a small carved stone on the side of the path. Kneeling down, he rubbed the moss off of a stone tablet.

Tracker ran his hand over the etchings. "It looks like a warning not to get off the path."

"What's it say will happen if we get off the path?" Raven asked.

"It doesn't say. The only thing on here other than the warning is an engraving of a tree and one of the fire lizards."

"Let me see that." Raven got in close. "That is the same tree I saw on fire in the crater."

Liney motioned them to keep going. "If we want to make the city before nightfall, we need to pick up the pace."

In six hours they reached a rock twice the size of a man which was cracked in two, leaving a path between the two pieces. When the three popped out the other end, they found themselves on the edge of the city.

"I have seen that rock a thousand times but never noticed a crack in it." Liney shook her head, looking at the rock.

That night they slept in the temple of the bear near the edge of the city. Early the next morning, they took the glow stones to the market to trade them for cloth and fittings for more kites. The air around them was filled with the scent of the fine ash. The first person they met was Joe, who ran the common market.

"I didn't expect to see you back, Raven." Joe smiled and held out his hand. "It's been a while since we've had glow stones to trade."

Raven handed him the bag with the five stones inside. "You've never seen any as large as these." She smiled.

Joe grabbed them and pulled the group into a doorway. "It's Lune coming around the corner." Joe put his finger to his lips. "This month she thinks she's a cat."

Joe shook his head. "Ever since they changed the law, things have gone off the deep end. It used to be kept private. Now it's all out in the open. If I choose to think I'm a cat, then I'm a cat. She could be an old man or a fish next month ... so don't suggest anything weird to her. She's quite impressionable."

"She's no different than the rest of the town." Raven looked to see Lune on all fours, meowing at shoppers. "A healthy imagination and a little bit of ash are a dangerous combination." Raven looked over at Joe. "You need to keep an eye on her. Now that I'm gone, she will kill herself if no one looks after her."

"Don't worry. If she starts acting like a bird, I'll give her an inside job." Joe smiled.

Raven half-smiled. "Thanks, Joe." She remembered how it was when she lived in the city. Lived in the ash cloud. There people chose their own reality, and in the cloud they came to really believe it. It wasn't such a bad deal for a time. The only unwritten rule was that one person couldn't challenge someone else's reality. It wasn't until she had built a community with the children that she understood the real downside of that rule. If everyone was living in his or her own reality and there was no challenging it, then there was no common reality to talk about. Conversation, and eventually thought itself, became shallow for fear of challenging someone else's reality. It was no wonder the children ran away into the woods. They were alone even when they were in a crowd. Everyone was. She was. With no common reality, one could be whatever one wanted to be, but one could never share it with someone else. One was a prisoner of one's own mind. Now she had real friends in Tracker and Liney and the children. She could never come back and live in the ash.

"World to Raven." Tracker waved his hand over her face. "Are you already lost in the ash?"

Raven gave Tracker a hug. "Just thinking, Tracker." *A novelty in this world*, she thought.

They completed their business with Joe and quietly made their way to the main path back to the western side of the island. They would have to make good time to get out of the woods before dark, and then they would have another full day to the cliff.

"I hate this part." Liney rubbed her eyes and adjusted the pack on her back filled with kite supplies. "Even if you're there only for a day, you get the headache coming out."

"Not good." Tracker rubbed his forehead and chewed on more uba leaves he had brought.

They reached the edge of the forest at dusk. As they were putting up their shelter for the night, there was a rustling at the tree line.

Raven pulled out her knife and slowly moved toward the noise. With a great rush, a dim yellow mass leaped out of the bushes. "It's Charlie!"

Charlie wagged his tail wildly, uprooting small bushes and trees. He then rolled onto his side for a belly rub.

"That's a good boy." Raven rubbed his scaly belly with both hands, taking care not to get in the way of the tail.

CHAPTER 23

KITE THIEF

THE NEXT MORNING, THEY took off early. It took most of the day to hike back to the cliff where they had left their kites. From a distance, Raven could see someone lying on the ground near their kites. If he meant to steal their kites, he had another think coming. She picked up her speed to a full run, leaving tracker and Liney behind. Charlie's nostrils filled with smoke, and his eyes turned from a deep blue to a fiery red. He ran shoulder-to-shoulder with Raven. In full sprint, she pulled out her knife from the sheath on her back. Only steps away, she let out a battle cry, raising the knife high. Charlie raised his mouth to the sky, and fire filled the air above. The man jumped to his feet with his arms stretched out. Only feet away, Raven stopped in her tracks, frozen by shock. Charlie dug his feet into the dirt only a foot from the man, looking to Raven for a signal as to what to do. Raven's knife dropped to the ground with her hand still held high in the air.

"Raven?" Redd took a hesitant step forward, his face lost in the moment.

Without thinking, she grabbed him in an embrace that had waited ten long years to be fulfilled. Tracker and Liney looked on. For what seemed an eternity, they exchanged stories and laughed and cried. The sun then rode low in the western sky, and Liney and Tracker tied a rope onto Redd and to both of their kites. Before Redd had time to properly protest the plan, he was dragged off the side of the cliff toward the second island.

Raven flew her kite down near Redd, banking left and right. Far below she could see Charlie swimming across the strait with his tail.

She could not remember being so happy. That day, she forgot about the burning tree.

A week later, Redd and Raven were married and moved to the third island to live with the children she had moved there. The wound on Raven's heel never fully healed. Like the burning tree, it passed out of the forefront of her mind and into the darker crevices from which stories are born.

CHAPTER 24

THE BLACK TUNNEL

Seventeen years later, in a small river valley in Tibet

JOHN LOOKED DOWN THE river that was rushing toward a massive hole in the earth. The older two children, Max and Mary, had already disappeared as rushing water carried them into the darkness of a tunnel that would lead them to the next black tree. Had he and the children not already been through one of these tunnels, he would have been nervous for the children. They had destroyed two of the black trees already. He wondered what type of monsters would guard the next tree. Franz, his youngest child, a boy of seven, zipped by him on the river toward the great hole. He seemed to have grown so much since John had taken the orphans into his home in the black forest of Germany. John watched as Franz dove high in the air with knives blazing in each hand. His voice bellowed into the waning light of day—a cry of war. Water rushed below him into a great hole that swallowed the river into the misty silence below. As John reached the dark tunnel that lay below, he wondered at how it absorbed all that entered with a deafening quiet.

Once in the tunnel, he began to pick up speed in free fall. He could feel the breeze pulling his hair back. The first time he fell through such a tunnel, he felt the fear of the unknown. As before, the tunnel began to glow red, and the wind that was ripping at his clothes grew hot and dry. The dampness from the river that had soaked his coat at the beginning now trailed behind him in a vapor trail like the tail of a comet soaring through the darkness of the void.

The red-hot glow of the tunnel soon gave way to a dull glow, and then the darkness returned. John wondered where the path would lead them next. He had given up second-guessing the narrow path. Thinking about anything other than the great bear, Soman, only served to slow one down. The path moved fast, and to stay alive one had to keep one's eyes ahead always. John now looked out into the darkness and saw small lights passing massive shadows in the distance. The breeze rushing against his face took on a salty feel, and soon he could make out fish swimming outside the tunnel wall. In the distance, he saw a great whale swimming to the left and then veering hard to the right, illuminated by a yellow glow that filled the sea. He seemed to be making his way toward the tunnel. He looked up and could see that Franz had his knives at the ready in each hand. Behind the whale, a dark shadow followed, rapidly closing in on the creature that was now frantically diving just in front of Franz. It was then that John saw the reason for the whale's rapid descent. White teeth three times the size of a man flashed by John in the blink of an eye. The light of the ocean grew dark for a moment as the shadow passed. Suddenly the shadow was gone, and John saw a portion of the whale floating in the water, bitten in half by the great beast that had given chase to it.

John looked up and could see the other end of the tunnel rapidly approaching, blue skies above. He looked back into the water just in time to see the great beast devour the other half of the whale whole. It flashed by the sidewall of the tunnel, and its two yellow eyes, which dwarfed John, looked at him and through him. John was tossed high in the air. Below he could see Franz, Max and Mary already bobbing in the churning sea. John felt weightless as he made the shift from upward to downward flight. As he dropped into the tormented waters of the sea, he could see an enormous black mass moving toward his family. Below he could see Franz diving under the water with his knives out before him. When John plunged into the water, he saw the two massive yellow eyes of the monster that had eaten the whale. The dark black scales of its lips pulled back to reveal row upon row of teeth that shone like sharp pillars in a row in a great hall. John's eyes were drawn toward a gap in the teeth where one appeared to be missing, and he smiled at the sight. With that the eyes disappeared, and John felt himself hurled into the air before landing hard on an island of dark shield-like scales that quickly made their way across the sea. Sitting beside him were Mary, Max, and Franz, who had been strewn haphazardly about on the dark isle.

Franz stood tall and wrapped his toes onto the side of one of the cold, dark scales as he raised a knife to the sky and slashed across the purple blue surface. The knife sunk deep into the rocklike scale, creating a hiss of white smoke. What followed felt like an earthquake as the island shook. Off in the distance, the massive head of a dragon erupted from the ocean and sped toward the party as fast as the wind. The beast's two yellow eyes looked down on Franz.

"Do not test me, little one." The great serpent tilted his head toward Franz. With one of the horns on top of his head, he pulled back Franz's cloak to reveal his leather breastplate emblazoned with the golden emblem of the bear. "So you are in the service of the bear." The beast snorted, blowing a small stream of fire from his nostrils. The fire licked the scale that Franz had cut, mending it seamlessly. "As are we all, whether we want it or not." The great serpent then raised its head so high in the sky that his eyes could only be seen from the bright light that shone from them.

From above John heard his voice like thunder from the clouds. "I am the most fearsome creature ever created. I have owned the seas since the world was new. I have been bidden by the Old One to give you passage to the five isles." The beast's head then shot down from the sky like a bolt of lightning, stopping just over their heads. "But the manner of delivery was not specified. Perhaps a pile of ash sprinkled among the islands." Leviathan looked Franz over with a smile as smoke seeped from his nostrils. His head then tilted suddenly as if he was listening to something in the distance.

It was a moment before John could hear a whistling in the wind that sounded like a faint song. He looked out to the open sea, and in the distance he could see a white bear jumping from wave to wave on the horizon.

Mary yelled, "It's Soman on the water."

Leviathan whipped his head back and gave them a menacing glare. "That is not the bear you seek." He paused for a moment, as if in deep thought. "I will deal with you momentarily. For now I will leave you safely treading water." Leviathan's head plowed back under the water.

Moments later, the island of scale that the party was sitting on slowly sank into the sea.

The water was now calm, and they were alone except for the image of the white bear, who appeared to be heading straight at them. John treaded water as fast as he could. His heavy clothing hung from his arms. Each stroke seemed smaller than the last as he began to bob in and out of the water. They would not last long like this. His eyes grew wide as the white bear leapt from wave to wave, closing fast. He took in a deep breath as the bear sped by, followed by a blur of gray and blue. John could make out the outline of a ship passing him by that blended in seamlessly with the waves. As the ship passed them, a door opened in the back of the boat, and out popped a rowboat with a man at the oars. The little boat skipped on the water as it slowed down from its escape and then began to turn toward the flailing swimmers.

"Grab onto the oar and climb in!" Yelled a man who was now waving frantically. He looked to one side and then the next, as if expecting to be ambushed at any time.

Franz was the first to get to the boat and climbed aboard. He then helped the others roll in. John was the hardest. Franz's eyes bulged as he pulled on his soaked sleeves. John thought to himself that he would need to go on a diet. He then smiled and laughed at the idea. The party lay strewn about the boat, fully exhausted.

As John caught his breath, he looked up to the tall blond stranger that had just saved him. "There is a monster in the water."

The man looked at him and nodded. He put down the oar he had used to fish them out of the water and picked up a black axe and a large gold ring. The man looked down at John's halberd as if studying the weapon. "Where did you get such weapons? Have you been on the *Eros* before?"

John looked at him with a puzzled expression. "We are in the service of the great bear." John lifted up his halberd, showing its spear tip and the axe head at the end of the shaft just underneath. "These were given to each of us in his service."

The blond man pointed his axe at John and brushed his beard to the side to see an emblem of the bear on his leather breastplate. He nodded. "Heavy clothing for fighting on the sea."

It was then that John noticed the strange armor on his body. The man was wrapped in leather straps with blades coming out of his elbows and knees. The man then shifted to the left, looking out. The water about them began to foam. *Eros* had made a full circle and was now coming back straight at them. As she approached, Leviathan's head exploded out of the water, rising into the heavens. John then saw the sky turn red and orange with flame as the head of the beast came crashing down. It was only then that he realized that they were bait being used to lure these sailors into a trap. *Eros* now was nearly upon them. John fixed his eyes upon the long spear coming out from her bow. He looked up at the tall man who had saved them. He appeared to have gone mad, as he was staring down the spear that was sure to pierce him in the head in only moments. John yelled and reached forward to pull the man away. The ship shifted slightly to the right, guiding the bouncing spear just past the man's head, where it entered the golden ring in his hand. John looked down into the boat as loops of rope disappeared behind the gold ring. He could now feel the heat above. There he could see no cloud or sky—only fire. They would surely die.

The rope suddenly grew taught, and a great wave lifted the rowboat into the air. Before John could contemplate what had happened, he found himself on the deck of a sailing ship. As the wind filled the sails above, the crew held on tight as *Eros* sped forward faster than the wind. The fireball ballooned out behind them and was followed by a giant wave.

Leviathan's head reemerged out of the deep and shot back up into the clouds behind them. As it disappeared behind them, she roared with anger, "We will meet again, little one."

The tall blond man looked down at Franz. "How did you get out in the middle of the sea?"

Franz pointed to the emblem of the bear on his breastplate. "We are in the service of the bear. He has called us to destroy the great black trees. He has brought us to you."

John was now standing just beside him. "That beast mentioned five islands nearby. Do you know of a black tree on those islands?"

The man looked at him and shook his head. "Those islands are cursed; there is little good you will find on them."

John looked at Franz and nodded.

The man looked at John for a moment and laughed. "*Eros* will take us where we need to be. If those islands hold your tree, you will find it soon enough." The man extended his hand. "My name is Tom."

John shook his hand, introducing himself and his companions. "Once we get to the islands, we may need a guide." John smiled, as did the rest of his party.

"I don't know all five of the islands well, but I do know someone who does. She may be able to help you. It has been many years since I have seen her. I knew her only when I was a child. But she is almost certainly on the middle isle by now—a very difficult place to get to."

Max stood tall, facing the horizon, and then turned to Tom. "Getting to difficult places is our specialty."

CHAPTER 25

NIGHTTIME STORIES

JOHN JOINED THE MEN on the main deck that evening as they roasted fish and told stories around the fire. He sat down next to Tom, grabbed a stick, and stuck it into a fish. He then held it over the fire and turned it slowly.

Tom turned to John. "Finding you and your children in the middle of the ocean is unbelievable. We would like to hear how you came to be here."

The men around the fire nodded. John twisted his fish one more time and then brought it up for a bite. "Not too long ago, I lived in a large house in a place called the black forest." John stuck the fish back into the fire. "I lived alone. My wife had died some years before, and I had almost gone mad with grief. It was then that the bear first came to me in my dreams. I didn't know him as I know him now. Back then I was afraid ... and lonely. One day I decided not to live alone anymore and rode into town to adopt some children to live with me at my farm. That is how I came to have Mary and Max, who are twins now in their teens, and their little brother Franz."

John laughed as he took another bite of fish. "I still remember how Franz looked the first time I saw him. His hair was so wild, he looked like a bush running about. We lived at my farm for several months. But even with their company, I still had the dreams—the dreams of the bear. In the middle of the winter, a catastrophic fire burned down my house. I nearly burned alive getting Franz out. It was then that the bear saved me."

John stared into the fire. "He saved me from myself. He showed me who he really was and who I was. It was then that he taught me to hear the song."

Tom chewed on a piece of fish and threw the skeleton into the fire. "What song was that?"

John turned and looked into Tom's eyes. "The song of the bear sustains all things ... creates all things ... holds all things together." John grabbed another fish and brought it up in front of Tom's eyes. "Watch the fish closely, Tom, as you listen to the song that sustains all things."

Tom watched and listened. "I can hear something faintly in the background of my mind." Tom then stared at the fish as if in a trance.

Tom sat silent for a moment after John took the fish away. He then turned to John and said, "At first the fish was as I have always known it. But then I saw it disappear and reappear like an illusion. It was like the fish was remade moment by moment as you passed it by."

"That was no illusion, Tom. That was the song. The song creates and sustains all things on a moment-by-moment basis—even your body, Tom. And it is the great bear, Soman, that sings that song. All things owe their continued existence to him."

Tom smiled. "I have met the bear. He led me out of the ash city."

John nodded. "Soman has been leading us all since the beginning. When you learn to lose yourself in him ... you are able to run the narrow path."

"The narrow path? What's that?"

"On the narrow path you live moment by moment. In a way, you become one with the bear—he in you, you in him. You are free to be your true self. You step out of the illusion of control. It is through the narrow path that you step into relationship with the bear—into adventure itself."

Tom grabbed another fish. "I used to know someone that spoke of freedom like you. What you speak of is not so different from how we live on the *Eros*." Tom nodded toward Mary and Max, who were sitting across the fire, talking to a few of the crew. "They look like they would be handy in a fight."

John nodded. "Mary has a sword that has a mind of its own, and Max is very handy with a bow. They fight together as if they were tied together with a string."

Tom looked over at Max's bow. "Your weapons have the same dark wood that our weapons are made from."

John picked up his halberd and ran his hand along the smooth surface of the shaft. "This wood comes from a black tree that was cursed. There are six in all. We have fought beasts you could not imagine in order to destroy two of the trees. Soman has sent us on a quest to destroy all six of the trees."

Tom pointed his stick at a young boy with wild, bushy hair near the fire. "What of the little one? Is he much of a burden on your quest?"

John laughed. "Franz a burden? He is the fiercest of all. He stood fast against a charging hoard of giant monsters. Don't worry about Franz. He can take care of himself."

Tom leaned back on a barrel. "So you are looking for a black tree. I have never seen such a thing on the islands. That may be a difficult task."

John leaned back himself. "Finding the tree is not the problem. The narrow path will lead us there. It's what's around the tree that's the problem. These trees tend to be surrounded by trouble."

CHAPTER 26

A VISIT FROM AN OLD FRIEND

THEY HAD NOW SPENT several days on *Eros*, sailing the open sea. Max nodded to Mary, who was leaning against her sword while looking out into the water. "I never dreamed there could be so much water in one place."

Max got up and looked over the side. "It goes on forever." The sun had not yet risen, and the rest of the ship lay sleeping. Max heard the deck panels creak behind him and turned to look.

"Good morning, Max," said Soman, who was now sitting behind them, eating a fish out of a bucket.

At his voice, Mary and Max leaped toward him and fell into his arms. Soman, the great bear, hugged them and held them tight as they wept.

Mary was in tears. "Where have you been? Will you be with us now for a while?"

Soman smiled and brushed her hair back. "I am always with you, child, even when you do not see me."

Max looked up. "That monster you sent to save us in the sea nearly burned us alive." Max's eyes grew wide. "She cannot be trusted."

Soman laughed and rubbed Max's head with his paw. "She can be trusted to play her part in this great adventure the Old One has prepared for us. She is no plaything to be trifled with. We each do our part in the adventure, whether we take joy in it or not."

"Did you see fear in the eyes of my men here on this ship when the fire rained from the sky?" Soman smiled and wiped a tear from Max's eye.

Max thought for a moment, as if replaying the scene in his mind. "No." He sat quiet for a moment. "Their eyes were filled with joy ... and anger. They were itching for a fight."

"They have lost many friends to Leviathan. There is a darkness in that beast's heart that was placed there long ago." Soman leaned in close as if to tell them a secret. "They can sense the evil in Leviathan, just as they can with the rest of the sea monsters that roam these waters. It fills their hearts with a righteous anger to rid the world of these evil beasts." Soman was quiet for a moment. "But it is not an anger that causes rash action. It is calculated and slow to rise, for its source is not a hunger for vengeance but instead a love for something larger. It has driven fear from their minds. They still feel the fear in their heart, but instead of controlling them, it excites the heart and pushes them farther into the moment … and that is where they find me, Max." Soman smiled. "I am in the hearts of all men and women who are in the moment, that sliver of space between past and future. It is there that men find courage, and it is through courage that we rise above the fears of our circumstances and begin to enjoy the adventure of the moment."

Mary smiled. "We love you, Soman. We want to live like that—to live without fear."

"You and Max are well on your way." Soman laughed. "Some of these men have served on *Eros* for over ten years. With time you will find the freedom to find joy in the moment. You will sense me there. You will not lose your fear. The Old One put it there for a reason. But it will not own you. You will use it as it was intended to be used—to drive you closer to me. When your mind is still, search your heart for its most intense desire. When all you see is my face, you will know that you are close. But beware of your heart, for like all hearts, it is treacherous. Your heart will only obey its deepest desire. By examining what you are obedient to, you will open a window into your heart and see it as it really is."

Max turned his head toward a noise from the ship's stern. In the distance he could see Tom sitting over the back of the ship, throwing fish heads into the water.

Soman then pulled them back close into him. His voice became hushed and very serious. "Do not forget why it is that we are here. The third tree can only be found by a woman named Raven. Her time in this world is growing short. She is very sick, but she holds within her my spirit, which is keeping her alive for this one last adventure. She will lead you through the water to the place of the tree, but she must first be made stronger. There is a forest on the large island under a cloud of ash that you must take her to, to make her strong. One of mine will find you there. But beware of the ash, and do not linger within it for longer than need be." Soman then rose up and looked to the stern of the ship.

"*Eros* is driven by the wind, and the wind is but a manifestation of my song that creates and sustains all things. When the Old One wills it, she will take you to where you need to go." Soman patted *Eros*'s deck beneath him. "Her heart is pure. She knows who she serves." With that, Soman leaped to the quarterdeck and bounded at full speed toward the rear of the ship, where Tom was sitting alone, throwing fish heads into a school of sharks following in *Eros*'s wake. With one last bound, Soman jumped over Tom off the back of the ship. "Take care of them, Tom; they are mine." Soman smiled as he splashed into the school of sharks. The great fish swirled and frothed for a moment and then made a raft with their bodies to hold Soman just above the water's edge as they sped him away.

Max looked on with a surprised expression on his face as Soman disappeared into the horizon of the rising sun. It was then that *Eros* lurched forward, her sails now filled with the full force of the wind. Tom grabbed hold of the rail, nearly falling as *Eros* sped ahead. The ship filled with the shouts of the men, who had been woken by the sudden movement. *Eros* was on the hunt. The men strapped on their battle gear as the sails whistled a song of adventure above.

Max strapped on his quiver and grabbed his bow. He nodded to Mary, who was unsheathing her broadsword. She nodded back. They ran to the bow of the boat, and there was Tom, looking onward at five islands in the distance. John and Franz were soon at their side.

"We saw Soman. He was with us only moments ago." Mary motioned her sword to where Soman had been sitting.

"He told us we needed to find someone named Raven … that she knew where the next tree was."

Tom's eyes grew wide as Max spoke Raven's name. "How do you know of Raven?"

"Soman told us we must find her and make her well again … that she will find the tree for us through the water."

Tom said, "The five islands are approaching fast. *Eros* only gives you one chance. We'll have to hurry. Quickly, follow me." Tom motioned them toward the rowboat. "John, loosen that rope over there." Tom pointed to a rope securing the rowboat to the mast. "We must get in the boat now."

The moment everyone was in the boat, Tom pulled a lever on the deck, and a trap door opened below. Their legs gave way beneath them as the rowboat slid down a chute and out of a window in the stern of *Eros*.

As the rowboat hit the water, the wind suddenly shifted, and *Eros* banked hard right, sending a massive wave toward the little boat, lifting it high above a row of sharp rocks near the shore and into a calm pool of water on the other side. Max looked over his shoulder and saw the jagged rocks behind them. He then looked below and saw the back current pulling them back toward the rocks.

Max grabbed both oars and rowed with all his might toward the beach beyond. They were losing ground until another giant swell lifted them again, this time onto the sandy beach of the island. In spite of the reef of death out toward the sea, the beach was calm, except for a large man riding a fire lizard toward them who appeared to be quite agitated.

CHAPTER 27

ON THE HUNT

Redd heard water crash upon rock in the bay. He had cursed those rocks when he was aboard the *Eros*, but he had come to appreciate them. They kept the larger sea beasts from coming in close to the island. But as of late, he had found the carcasses of smaller distorted sea creatures washing ashore, battered by the outer rocks. He was certain that it was a concerted effort from those foul beasts to invade the forest with their own kind. Another great wave hit the rocks. Redd looked down at Charlie, on whom he was mounted. Charlie looked up and nodded. Charlie took off like the wind toward the beach. Redd held on tight to a rope that he had fastened into a harness around Charlie's neck. As they broke through the edge of the forest, he could see something moving far down the beach. Redd spurred Charlie on as he lifted his black spear. Charlie sped down the beach, blowing fire. Red and orange flame hovered over the waves as they washed upon the sand.

In the distance, he could now make out what looked like a young boy leaping toward them with long hair as wild as the sea. Redd's mind raced as he tried to process what was going on. Was this a trick brought on by the beasts? A black dagger careened off of Charlie's head, whistling just past his ear. The thing that could be a boy then dug his feet into the sand only twenty yards away. Raising his knives high in the sky, he gave a great war cry. Charlie slid to a stop only feet away, raised his head, and blew a stream of fire high above the trees. He then lowered his head to look straight into the eyes of the thing that could be a boy and they were both silent for a moment. Franz then threw his knives into the sand and reached his hand out to Charlie, who turned his head slightly. Franz rubbed him behind the ear, and Charlie's tail waved back and forth in the wet sand.

Redd took his spear and, with the tip, pulled back a tuft of the wild hair of the boy to see a smiling face with eyes that had no fear. He had not seen that look in someone so young before. His trance on the boy was broken by the shout of one of the oncoming crew running across the beach.

"Redd?" Tom stopped in his tracks with his mouth hanging open.

Redd got off of Charlie and ran toward Tom. "Tom, is that you?" Redd grabbed Tom by the shoulder and looked into his eyes. "How can this be? How did you get onto this island?"

"*Eros* crested a wave over the barrier rocks, and we rode the rowboat over the top." Tom waved his hand back toward the rowboat that still had the dragon scales nailed onto its side, just as Redd had left it. "We are on a mission, Redd; we need to find Raven."

Redd felt a heaviness in his heart. "Raven is not well, Tom. She has not been well for several years."

"The great bear was on the *Eros*, Redd." Tom waved back toward the sea. "He told these travelers that Raven would help them find—"

Tom was interrupted by the sound of a whistle. Redd and the others turned and saw Max and Mary waving them to come quickly.

When everyone arrived, Max pointed the end of his bow to a large depression in the sand. "These tracks are fresh." Max pointed back to the waterfront. "Something must have been washed over the rocks with us from *Eros*'s wave."

Redd frowned. "I was afraid this would happen." Redd pointed out to the wall of jagged rocks in the water. "They have been trying to get through that for several years now. I have seen their torn bodies wash ashore. They are vile creatures—spawn of the sea beasts we fight on *Eros*." Redd shook his head. "I am sure by this time that the forest on the main island must be teeming with these beasts around the shallow, unprotected beach near the village. They could just roll ashore there."

Tom grabbed Redd's arm, pulling him out of thought. "We need to find Raven and bring her to the main island, Redd."

Redd shook his head. "First we need to kill whatever just crawled into my forest … then we will talk of Raven." Redd looked into the thick brush that the beast had squeezed through. If there was an opening, the forest had already closed it off. "The brush and thickets are too dense for us to follow the beast straight away. We will need to ride around the center of the forest and circle back the same way we came in. We can set a trap there and wait him out."

Mary shook her head. "That will take too much time." Mary took several steps to the forest's edge and unsheathed her sword. The sword moved here and there over the sand as if it had a mind of its own—which it did. Mary then closed her eyes and began to sing of her love of the bear.

Redd looked on as the rest of the party grabbed their weapons and made ready to leave in haste. It was then that, without a noise, the trees and brush opened before them. A path of soft earth lay ahead. Mary rushed in, followed by her friends.

Max turned back toward Redd as he ran forward. "Stay close, and do not fall behind. The path moves fast, and it never goes backward."

Redd mounted Charlie, looked at Tom, and shrugged, and they both took off after the rest. Once they were on the narrow path, it began to close behind them. Redd looked back and saw branch and limb and thick bunches of thorns all converging behind him. Unlike the path opening, the closing did make a noise—like that of grinding teeth. Tom asked, "What do you think happens if you get caught in that?"

Redd looked back and then picked up his pace. "I don't know, but it doesn't look good. We need to keep up, Tom." Several moments passed. "What I can't figure out is how we are going to find that beast moving at this pace over a path with no tracks. We could run right by him and never know better."

Franz suddenly popped out of the side wall of the path, flying over their heads like a squirrel moving through the trees. He sang smaller tunnels that opened just as it seemed he was about to crash into a wall of thorns and branches. "Trust in the narrow path. It will take you to where you need to be." Franz disappeared from sight and then suddenly emerged from an opening in the trees ahead. "It will take you to where you need to be whether you want to be there or not."

At that moment, the path ahead opened into a clearing where a beast three times the size of Charlie turned toward them with a startled look. Its skin was gray with heavy green lines that accented its many wrinkles. Its head was heavy with bone and a jaw that looked as if it could snap a man in half with no effort. That head turned toward Mary, who had already braced herself for the charge. A crater of ash erupted on the beast's side as one of Max's arrows found its mark. John did not break stride as he charged the beast head-on with his halberd already in backswing. Franz flew high over him with two knives in hand, landing lightly on the beast's head.

Redd had been in many battles but had never seen a crew attack a beast so quickly. He kicked at the side of Charlie, who charged ahead. In front of him he saw Mary duck left as her blade cut deep through the lower jaw of the beast. A piece of flesh and bone the size of Mary herself fell to the ground with a thud. The beast then shifted its weight left as John's halberd found purchase in its front right leg, cutting clean through. Redd charged Charlie straight into what was left of the beast's face as he ran his spear into one of its eyes. A hiss of smoke and ash erupted from the resulting crater. Franz then crawled over the beast's head and tapped the blade of his knife over his eye as if to complement Redd on his marksmanship. He then drove his blade into the beast's flesh just over its eye and swung into full view of the beast's remaining eye. The beast roared and lifted up on its hind legs, shaking its head wildly as Franz ran his blade into the eye. For a moment, Franz disappeared into a cloud of ash and smoke. He then swung in rhythm to the beast's flailing head flying high in the sky. With two blades in hand, he landed back on the beast's head and began digging into the skull.

The blind beast flailed wildly, knocking over trees as it hit the side of the clearing. Redd ran Charlie near the beast, and Charlie blew a stream of fire into one of Max's arrow craters on the beast's side. The whole beast then then glowed a fiery red, quivered for a moment, and fell lifeless to the ground.

Redd wiped his brow as he surveyed the clearing. The sun above reflected off the broad leaves of the forest that encased them in a thirty-yard circle. There was no way out. Charlie pawed at the trees. With his brute strength, he might be able to squeeze out, but no one would be able to follow. They were trapped. He looked over to Mary with a question in his eyes. Mary nodded back and approached the wall of trees. With her sword drawn, she began singing again, and just as before, the trees opened into a path. She charged in with the rest following close.

* * * * *

John brought up the rear. Just before he entered the path, a slight movement caught the corner of his eye. He slid to a stop just before passing beyond the wall of trees. He whistled hard as the trees closed up in front of him. That path was now closed. Seconds later, a small hole in the trees opened above, and out popped Franz, leaping down next to John.

John pointed toward the beast's carcass. Several sets of footprints led away from the beast's belly into the tree line. Franz nodded as John ran full speed toward the trees. He had a smile on his face but no song on his lips. The bear was now always on John's mind, superimposed on all that he saw. Just before he ran into the wall of the forest, it opened up, and Franz followed above on the path. John stood nearly seven feet tall. Despite his heavy build, his feet landed lightly on the soft dirt of the path as he ran full stride. He carried his halberd with both hands, always at the ready. The path suddenly opened. Two gray beasts with yellow stripes down their backs lumbered on a cleared path. They were the size of John and had the look of their mother. Ash and smoke exploded from one as Franz's throwing knives found their target. John swung his blade and beheaded the other beast without breaking stride. He jumped high as he hit the edge of the trees. The trees opened in rhythm to his movement as if they were happy to have him back within their realm. Franz bounced about from side to side up above, sometimes creating small tunnels that he would pop out of farther down the path, sometimes bouncing from wall to wall like a ball.

The path opened again with one of the beasts to John's left. His halberd fell heavy on its neck. He did not see the head fall before he again entered into the path. Franz howled with disapproval at John's quick dispatching of the beast. John had been chided before for killing more than his fair share of the beasts. John tipped a finger toward his eye in recognition of the constructive criticism leveled upon him. The path soon opened again with one last beast. It no sooner saw John than he was already at the other end of the clearing, opening the next path. John heard the hiss of smoke as Franz's knives flew into the beast. In the past he would have looked back to ensure the job was done, but no longer. Franz did not miss. They ran for another hour before the path emptied into the open land of the upper island. There, waiting for them off to the side, was the rest of their party.

John smiled as he wiped the dark blood from his blade in the grass. "Just cleaning up, Max." He glanced over and saw Redd prod Charlie with his heel and then take off across the grassy field.

CHAPTER 28

OF KITES AND SONGS

SEVERAL HOURS INTO THE journey, they came to a small village. There Tom greeted many of his childhood friends from the temple of the bear. They now had families of their own with small children running between the thatch huts that served as their homes. Redd paused for several moments to speak with one of the men and then waved the party forward. Far up the hill they could see a single house made of stone with smoke coming from a chimney.

As John approached the house, he felt a tinge of apprehension he had not felt since he had met Soman. Outside the house lay several kites covered by vines that had overgrown them in their years of disuse. The house had a dark look upon it. A vision of his barn with a wooden cow suspended by a rope overtook his mind. There was a tear in his eye as he entered the house. In the far end of the room, Redd was kneeling over Raven's bed. John's chest grew heavy, and his breaths short. He looked around him for a window, but they were all covered with heavy cloth. John backed up to the door and nearly fell out of the house as he made his way to fresh air.

Max came out and asked, "What's wrong, John? We are all in this together."

John nodded and looked up. Tears were now rolling down his cheeks. He straightened himself and looked down upon Max with a smile. "This all reminds me of Becky before she died. The house has the same feel." He patted Max on the back. "I'll be all right Max. I just needed some air."

They walked back into the room, and Redd introduced each one of them to Raven. Her cheeks were white and pulled tight across a face that found no joy. Her limbs were the color of dark ash, with skin pulled tight on bone. When John made his way to greet her, he knelt down with a smile and took her hand. It was cold. He had felt that before. She did not have much time left.

Max turned to Redd. "We need to get her to the forest on the main island."

Redd looked down at Raven and then back at Max. "Do you see what I see? To move her now would kill her."

"There is a man in the forest that will help heal her. Soman told us she must lead us to the tree." Max motioned Redd to pick Raven up, but Redd did not move. Max approached Raven, knelt down, and whispered something in her ear.

Raven stirred, opening her eyes. A faint request left her lips. "Let's go, Redd. If it's my time, then it's my time."

It was the first time that Raven had spoken in a week. Redd knelt down and brushed her hair back. They looked into each other's eyes, and he nodded. He then sprang to his feet, burst to the open door, and ran down to the village below. Moments later, the village stirred into life like a hornet's nest knocked one too many times. Shortly thereafter, men and women began climbing the hill toward the stone house, each carrying a kite and rope.

Redd ran ahead of the crowd and patted Max on the back. He then wrapped Raven tightly in a blanket and carried her out to the crowd. When the villagers saw Raven, they cheered. Redd looked over his shoulder at the setting sun. "We will have only a couple hours of sunlight left."

One of the men in the crowd looked up at Redd. "We will never make it to the big island before dark."

"We aren't going to the big island tonight. We just need to make it to the second island, and there we will have a place to stay for the night."

Redd turned to his new friends and smiled. A new fire burned in his eyes. "Let's get going."

It was an hour's walk to the edge of the cliff. John looked across the churning water far below that separated them from the far cliff of the second island. He looked about him and saw his friends being harnessed by the rope. Their intent was clear. They were going to jump off the cliffs with him tied to one of the kites. He took another look down the cliff. He chuckled to himself. For all the things that they had faced, to be nervous about jumping off a cliff? He would have none of that.

A small woman came up to John and handed him a rope. John looked over her small build. She smiled. "You are a big man, and I am the smallest kite flier. The kite can only hold so much weight." She patted his stomach. She then looked over the edge of the cliff. "With the help of the bear, we will make it across." A smile slid across her face that was less than reassuring.

John double-checked the rope tied around him. It was as tight as he could get it. All the others had already jumped and were slowly making their way across the chasm. John and the woman looked at each other. He finally motioned the woman to crawl up onto his back. He then lumbered back about twenty feet, took a deep breath, and started running. With his last step, the ground kissed him goodbye and they fell. John was not sure how this was supposed to go, but it seemed to him that they were falling at an excessively fast rate. He looked up at the woman, who gave him a thumbs-up. She looked straight ahead with no fear on her face.

It was then that the ropes grabbed hard, as if to remind John that he was still alive. He felt a slide to the left as the kite banked and began to pull them back up. John looked down at the water below. The sun was low in the sky, and the pink clouds above reflected throughout the channel, giving its deadly waters a soft and feathery feel. They banked right and then left again. Above he could see the other kites slowly making their way up on the updraft of the opposite cliff. John looked down at the frothy pink water. It was getting steadily closer. He could feel the updraft blowing on his arms. It was not going to be enough. He looked up at the woman with him. No words were said, but he saw in her face the truth. They would not make it up the other side.

She then dove down sharply. John felt as if the bottom had been taken out from underneath him. As John approached the water, it looked less friendly up close. The woman then pulled out of their dive. John could only guess it was one last attempt to harness the updraft to pull them up—but up they would not go. The water was now only inches below his feet. He began to run on what water his feet would touch as if that would help their cause.

Without warning, another kite banked hard and nearly clipped their wing as it then soared high above, somersaulted, and then dove again. Through the bushy hair of its passenger, he heard the battle cry of Franz. The kite flew hard and fast like Franz in the path, mimicking his squirrel-like jumping. John ran harder and began to hum the song of love of Soman that he had used at first to open the narrow path. At least he would go out with the great bear in the forefront of his mind and his heart. His strides grew long, and he began to feel the rhythm of the run. The kite above him suddenly found the strength it had so sorely lacked. John felt his feet pulled off the water with a force that took his breath away. The kite rose high and fast, passing Franz as a blur. John barely heard Franz's howl of approval as they sped up the side of the cliff. John was now singing as loudly as he could. He saw little other than Soman's face in his mind's eye as he sang louder and louder. The woman above looked down at John with wonder. With a swoosh, they overshot the edge of the cliff and flew high into the twilight of the sky. It was the most beautiful sight John had ever seen. Some two hundred yards above the cliff, he lowered his voice and the kite finally reached the apex of its climb. John then hung silently in wonder as the woman slowly brought them back down to the landing point and lightly landed them near the others.

Once they had landed, she looked at him with wide eyes. "What was that that you did?"

John smiled and wiped a drop of sweat from his brow. "When the night is quieter, I will explain what just happened."

John then felt a whoosh of air as Franz dive-bombed him, still on the kite. John motioned him to come down. Franz nodded, the kite banked hard, and in they came. Once they had landed, the kite flier and Franz jumped high and slapped his hand high over the others. John had not seen such a thing before, but he thought to himself that such a thing could catch on.

Franz's flier let out another yell at the sky and pointed down toward Franz. "Little man, I've got you on the next ride to the big island."

Franz tipped his knife blade to his eyebrow and smiled.

Up front, Redd had Raven over one shoulder and a kite over the other. He waved them forward. "Nice recovery, John." Redd smiled with a glow to his face. "We thought we had lost you. It seems your crew has some special skills."

CHAPTER 29

A PLAN IS HATCHED

THE FOLLOWING MORNING, THEY woke up at Liney and Tracker's house. It was a small house, and a lot of people were there. Redd looked around him. It looked as if a hurricane had passed through. Arms and legs hung down from every flat surface in the cabin. Looking out the window, he saw a stream of fire shoot across the meadow. Redd stepped out and found Charlie chasing Franz around the field. Redd smiled. It seemed that Charlie had found his match. Redd walked back into the cabin. "Time to get going. We have a long day ahead of us."

The tangle of arms and legs began to squirm to life. Tracker and Liney were already outside, prepping the kites for the next flight. Redd stepped back outside and found Tracker tightening the cloth on one of the kites.

Tracker gave the cloth a good tug. "Those kids need to bring the kites in a little more often." He laughed and began working on the next kite. "One of the travelers said you needed to get into the ash forest on the big island ... said there was a man in the woods that could heal Raven."

Redd looked back at the cabin. "We'll see ... the ash forest on the main isle is not an easy hike."

Tracker rubbed his head as if trying to remember something. "A long time ago, we found a path through the forest. It looked like it was made before we were born—a long time before. There is no way we could hit the top end of the path but we could come at it from the bottom." Tracker paused for a moment. "But that would mean going back through town."

Redd grimaced. He had not gone into town since he and Raven had moved to the third isle. He looked over at Charlie. The townspeople would not be okay with Charlie. They would need to have a plan. People were now piling out of the cabin, with Liney shoving food into their pockets and knapsacks as fast as she could. Liney was dressed to fly. Redd looked over to Tracker. "Where does Liney think she's going?"

Tracker laughed. "You can't find the path on your own, Redd. Besides, it's time we got out and stretched our legs."

Redd smiled. "It would be good to have some company." Tracker said, "She's our friend too, Redd. We will see this thing done. Besides, if you want to take Charlie with you, you will need a plan. And I just happen to have such a plan."

Liney came up from behind them with a pile of blankets sewn together in what looked like a giant dress. "Throw this on Charlie. We'll put it on him later." Redd thought she must be crazy. Liney pushed the blankets at Redd. "Just do as I say, Redd. The city people have one *huge* weakness. They won't say a thing." Liney turned away to grab her kite. "It's gotten worse since you've been there, Redd. No one will say anything."

Redd whistled Charlie over and laid the blankets on his back. John brought Raven out and placed her on Charlie. With that, the party took off toward the other end of the isle.

Several hours later, they reached the outer cliffs of the second isle. Across the chasm, Redd could see the main isle. Charlie was the first to jump off the cliff into the foamy water below. Redd saw him hit the water, and with one tail wag into the foam, he was gone. Normally fire lizards stayed out of the deeper water, but Charlie seemed to love it. The next off the cliff were John and his kite flier. Redd watched as the kite soared high into the air, propelled by who knew what. There was something about John. He seemed to be followed by a favorable wind wherever he went. It would be good to have him close. Franz and his flier were the next to go. Their kite flew high into the air and did a full loop. Redd had never seen that before. Having watched Franz jump in the field, he wondered if the boy even needed a kite to cross the channel. The men on the *Eros* must have loved him. Redd took off with the rest of the crew, with Raven tied securely to his back. She had been quiet on the trip so far. He hoped she would make it. Once they all landed on the far side, they tied down the kites. The villagers made camp with the kites.

John looked over at Redd and pointed toward the villagers. "They look like they would be pretty handy in a fight. Don't you want them to come along?"

Redd shook his head. "The fewer the better in town. When we get to town, stay close. It will get a little weird."

CHAPTER 30

THE CITY OF ASH

TWO DAYS LATER, THEY reached the edge of town. They had chewed on uba leaves the entire way, preparing for the ash. Redd dismounted Charlie but left Raven on his back. Liney moved Redd to the side and threw the giant blanket dress over Charlie, covering Raven underneath. She tied a large bonnet over Charlie's head. Charlie looked over at Redd as if to protest the situation.

Redd looked at Charlie and then over to Liney. "This is never going to work. No one is going to believe that this is Raven."

Liney gave Redd a stern look. "Raven believes she is a giant fire lizard ... that is what Tracker is telling the city people right now."

Redd nodded and started to lead Charlie into town. As he walked down through the city, everyone stayed clear. All around him, things lay strewn on the street. Shop signs hung lopsided off of buildings that had needed to be repainted ten years ago. Garbage lay all around, with some of the townspeople sleeping on the curb. Redd made way for a man running down the middle of the street, waving his arms wildly. The man came close to Redd and made a swishing sound with his mouth and then moved on. Redd looked over to Liney with one eyebrow raised.

"He thinks he is the wind, Redd. That is his chosen reality. He is mostly harmless unless he chooses to storm."

"What?" Redd's eye was then caught by a woman in a window jumping about and throwing plates at someone else in the room that evidently was not enjoying her reality.

"Don't stare or make eye contact, Redd." Liney picked up her pace. "She chose to be a monkey nearly a year ago. That was a tough run of luck for her husband."

Redd heard a man in the house yell out in pain. "What is going on here, Liney? What happened to the city?"

"The ash has been falling more heavily over the last several years. It has fully saturated their minds, Redd. They think they can choose whatever personal reality pops into their head. Old men decide they are young girls, young girls decide they are potted plants, our lady back there decides she is a monkey. There is no limit to the madness, Redd. The city is falling apart."

Redd looked around him. "I guess no one around here chose to believe he is a repair man."

"Don't say that too loud, Redd. The only taboo left in the town is the prohibition against challenging someone else's reality. That's why Charlie is able to walk down the middle of town without anyone saying a thing. If Raven chooses to be a giant fire lizard, then so be it. If you challenge someone's personal reality, the whole community will come down on you like a load of bricks." Liney looked up at the road ahead. "There's the rock I told you about."

Redd looked over and saw the same large rock at the edge of town that he had seen since he was a child. Tracker was up ahead near the rock, and then he was gone. Redd tilted his head, not believing what he saw. One by one, the rest of his party disappeared into the rock. When he arrived, he could see the crack in the shadow. "How could this have stayed secret for so many years?" He then looked back toward town and nodded. He looked over to Liney. "This is evil, Liney. Look at what it has done to the city. John thinks that somehow this is all being caused by a giant black tree. We need to help him find this thing and kill it."

Liney nodded as she disappeared into the rock. Redd lifted Raven off of Charlie and took off his blanket dress and threw it into the brush. "This crack is too narrow for you, boy. You will need to find a way around."

Charlie wagged his tail and bolted off into the forest as Redd slipped through the crack with Raven on his shoulder.

Liney was already leading the group up the forest path when Redd got through. The path was covered under the forest's canopy. Getting out of the sun felt good. Charlie quickly found his way around. They were a good two hours up the path when Liney stopped. She bent down and looked about the ground. Redd could see nothing about this part of the path that was any different from any other part of the path. He patted Charlie on the head to get him to stop.

"There was a side path around here somewhere." Liney waved at the dark forest to her side. "If there is someone living in the ash forest, we will not find them staying on this path. We have taken it all the way to the top of the mountain."

Redd looked over to Mary, who unsheathed her sword and approached the forest's edge. She then began to sing, and the forest opened before them into a narrow path. Mary sprinted ahead with the rest of the group close behind. Tracker pulled up the rear with Redd. The sound of crunching limbs and branches closing behind them drove them forward.

Tracker picked up the pace. "What happens if we fall behind on this thing?"

Redd did not look back. "Not good. Keep running."

Redd had lost track of time when the path opened into a small clearing still covered by the canopy of the forest. In the middle of the clearing sat a small mill with a brook that ran underneath and around it. The whole party stood looking at the building with only the sound of the water rushing over rock to remind them that it was not a dream. Redd took Raven from Charlie's back and carried her to the front door, which opened as he approached. Standing in the doorway stood a man with a silvery beard, his hands stretched out toward them.

The man took one step down and motioned Redd to give him Raven. "I have been waiting for you, Redd." The man pulled back the blanket and looked at Raven's ashen face. "She is almost gone." He turned with Raven and started to head back into the house. Everyone began to follow behind. He turned his head and spoke to Redd in a low voice. "Just you and Raven. Everyone else stays outside." Redd explained the situation to his friends and slipped into the house.

Raven opened her eyes and asked, "What am I doing here?

The silver-haired man smiled. "You're dying. We are about to change that. The great bear still has work for you to do."

Raven laughed until she coughed. "I can barely breathe. I'm not in a position to help anyone."

The man smiled and tapped her forearm. He frowned for a moment. Reaching to his right, he took a silver needle connected to a tube that hung from the ceiling. "The poison from the sea beast has saturated your body." The man gently inserted the needle into Raven's arm. Redd jerked forward but the man motioned Redd to remain where he was. A red fluid began to flow through the tube. Raven immediately began to shake. The man gave her a piece of soft wood to bite down on.

The man looked down on her with a concerned smile. "This can get a little rough." The man then motioned Redd to take Raven's other arm, and together they lowered her through an opening in the floor, fully submerging her in a brook that ran beneath the house.

Raven looked up at the men through the water. Her whole body shook violently. Her eyes were now wide open.

After a minute, Redd looked over to the man. "She's drowning. We need to lift her up!"

The man shook his head. "Not yet, Redd. Just a little while longer. You will know when it's time."

Raven pulled hard at the men's grip, nearly bringing them both into the water. One of her legs drifted down in the water. Redd could see her foot brace firmly on the creek bed. He readied himself.

Raven shot out of the water like an explosion, throwing the two men to the floor. She landed on her feet like a cat itching for a fight.

The man looked to Redd and smiled. "That's how you know it's time, Redd."

Redd saw Raven frantically look to her left and right. She looked like a wild animal. "Raven, it's Redd. We're here to help." Raven turned toward Redd with a blank stare. Redd could then feel her eyes meet his. She ran to him and held him firmly in her arms.

"Raven ... you are healed!" Redd let out with what little air was left in him. Raven let up on her embrace, and he took a deep breath.

* * * * *

Stepping away, Raven looked at her body. It was as it had been twenty years ago. She flexed her fingers, feeling the strength of her grip. It felt strange, as if there were no resistance to hold her back in this world. She then turned toward the man who was tying off the red line. "How is this possible?"

"All things are possible through the great bear, Raven. You still have unfinished work in this world ... but what we have done will not last long. You have a week to complete the task you were made for, but then you will return to the world from which you came."

Raven gave the man a confused look. "What unfinished work?"

The man arose and opened the door. He hugged Raven as she stepped outside to meet the gasps and cheers from the small crowd that ran close to meet her. The man pointed to a boy in the crowd. "Max will let you know what you need to do." The man kissed Raven on the forehead. "May the strength and peace of the bear follow you to whatever end he has planned for you."

Tears came to Raven's eyes as everyone came close. Raven turned her eyes to Max. "The man in the house told me that you know what I need to do ... some sort of task."

Max came in close. "Soman, the great bear, told me that you would lead us to the black tree."

Raven stepped back for a moment as her eyes glazed over. "I know of this tree. I saw it deep within the crater that smokes at the top of that mountain." Raven pointed up the mountain. "But there is no way we could go down into that crater from the top. It is filled with ash and smoke. We would surely die."

Max was silent for a moment as if in deep thought. "Soman said that you would lead us through the water. I don't think that would mean we would approach the tree through the top of the mountain."

Raven nodded. "Many years ago, we went to the top of that mountain. There we saw steps that had been carved into the rock. I have seen steps like those on the fifth island going down into the water."

Redd handed Raven a broadsword with a black handle very similar to Mary's sword. "The man in the house said you would need this."

Raven took the sword. She whipped it around as if it were as light as a feather. She swung it through the air, but in midswing it stopped suddenly with a clang of metal on metal as Mary met Raven's blade with her own. Mary smiled and twirled with her blade, aiming a blow at Raven's legs. Raven's blade seemed to come alive, shifting like lightning to parry the blow. Mary again twisted and aimed a blow at Raven's chest. Raven's sword again came alive, deflecting the blade high into the sky.

Mary laughed. "That is a very special sword you have there. You will need to learn to trust it."

Raven looked puzzled. Mary then slowly held out her blade so Raven could touch it. Raven ran her thumb hard over the blade. "It is dull." She ran her thumb over her own blade. "It won't even cut my thumb."

Mary smiled. "That is because it was not designed to cut your thumb. When evil presents itself, you will see the edge of the blade come alive."

Raven turned toward Redd. "What did the man tell you in the doorway?"

Redd picked up his hooked spear from the ground. "He said the narrow path will never give you more than you can handle, but it will give you all that you can handle." He then paused. "He said that we could handle quite a bit. He said to keep an open eye."

They were all already walking to the forest's edge. Raven looked to Redd. "What's the narrow path?"

Redd smiled and nodded to Mary, who made ready with her sword and began to sing. The forest opened, and off they ran. Raven stayed close to Redd. She looked back at the path closing in and gave Redd a questioning look. He spurred her on to pick up the pace. "They say it stops for no one and that it never goes backward. We need to keep up."

* * * * *

Back at the cottage, the man followed the red line along the ceiling into a back room. There he pulled the line from Soman's arm and helped him out of the brook in which he was sitting. Blood from the line dripped into the water. The fish that had gathered around Soman grew a full inch as they came in contact with the blood.

The man let the line drip, watching the fish grow as he looked on. "I can't believe Redd did not recognize me." He paused for a moment in thought. "Why not tell her how this ends? It would relieve some of the anxiety, don't you think."

Soman reached down into the brook with his paw and scooped out two large fish, tossed them into the air, and swallowed them whole. "This life must be lived to the end. Such words are hard to absorb, even if they come from me." Soman raised his paws and gave praise to the Old One for the fish provided, and then he scooped out two more. "Were her eyes full of life when she came out of the water?"

The man continued to clean up. "She looked like she was going to explode with life."

Soman laughed while he reached down and grabbed another fish. He handed it to the man and then slapped him on the back. "I hope they enjoy their adventure. A life without adventure is a wasted life. We can only hope that they will see it as it is so that they may enjoy it."

"Do you think she will?"

"I have already planted the seed. The little wild one you saw near the forest's edge—he will show her in a way that only he could."

"The little one, huh? He didn't look like much."

Soman let out a great belly laugh. "The evil on this island will soon feel my wrath through that little one. You will see it before the end."

The man shook his head. "I still can't believe that Redd did not recognize me. We spent nearly ten years together on the *Eros*. How could he not?"

"Tanner, ten years with me will change a man—how he acts ... how he looks. Redd will know you before the end." Soman rubbed his back and pulled him in tight.

Tanner reached over to a chest and pulled out another long sword. He swung it one way and then another with such grace that one could imagine it was a part of his body. "My time grows short. I'm anxious to move on."

Soman pulled him in close. "Your time has come. Your long fight in this world grows close to an end. Your last path will be with my friends."

CHAPTER 31

DINNER WITH A FRIEND

RAVEN AND HER PARTY ran through the forest into the evening. As the sun gave up the last of its light upon the land, they came to a large clearing in the forest. The tightly knit trees made a perfect circle in the forest. High above, the stars shined bright, inviting them to rest. Raven gathered wood from the clearing and piled it into the center of the circle. Charlie needed no prompting to breathe fire into the tower of wood, which immediately roared to life in yellow and orange flames. All around, Raven could see flowers blooming from the trees that separated them from the dark of the forest.

Suddenly Franz bounded close to her. Franz smiled and walked in close to Raven and motioned her to bend over. He leaned in close to her ear and whispered, "Catch me if you can." Raven then jumped high as Franz's blade nicked her in the backside. She took off toward Franz, who was heading to the perimeter of the circle with the two bags in his hand. As she followed, he jumped high in the air, catching a limb fifteen feet above. Keeping in rhythm, he landed on another limb in front of and above him.

Raven did not hesitate; she leapt after him from one limb after another. The pair looked like two squirrels chasing each other up a spiral. The flowers from the trees brushed across her face as she raced across the branches, perfuming her body with the beauty of the forest. The next branch dipped with her weight as she landed. She was now at the top of the canopy, one hundred feet high. Seeing how high she was on such a small branch, she grabbed a nearby branch to steady herself. The smell of the flowers surrounded her as she looked up into the night sky. The peace of the moment overtook her, and she began to weep. It was then that she felt her branch dip ever so slightly. Through her teary eyes, she saw Franz holding out a mango for her to take. He had peeled half and already taken a bite. She took the mango from his hand and took a huge bite. She felt the goodness of the fruit rush through her as the juice dripped down her chin. She handed it back to Franz, and together they shared a meal with no words spoken. When they were done, Franz threw what was left into the fire below and handed one of two bags to Raven. He then springboarded off the branch to another, grabbed several mangoes, and placed them into his bag. He looked back to Raven and made a motion with his head for her to follow.

Raven looked down, took a deep breath and jumped. In midair a breeze caught her and ruffled her hair. She did not look down but only to the next branch. Soon she was hopping from limb to limb, gathering fruit. Minutes later, each was holding a full bag of fruit. No word needed to be spoken. Franz gave her a nod, and the race was on to the bottom.

CHAPTER 32

FLYING SOLO

THE NEXT MORNING, THE party awoke to a sky on fire with pink and white clouds. They packed up and made haste on the narrow path, which led them up the mountain. Raven followed Franz closely on the path, jumping from side to side. Even when Franz would sing a side tunnel into the path, she would follow—sometimes on her hands and knees, as Franz's tunnels were not very large. It was midday when they reached the edge of the forest not far from the cliff where the villagers waited with the kites.

When the villagers saw Raven, they broke out in cheers. Everyone ran to touch her, not believing it could be Raven. After she and Franz had told of what had happened to them, they moved to the cliff side. Redd carried over an old green kite that they had taken with them and handed it to Raven. It was her old kite. She strapped it on tight as she watched Franz in the distance speaking with one of the villagers. The man waved and walked away somewhat deflated. It was the villager that had flown over with Franz. Franz bounded over to Raven and handed over the rope she would carry him with.

"Today we fly together." Franz tied the rope tight and pointed toward the cliff.

Raven looked over to her right and saw John tied up with Redd. She gasped. She began to sidestep over to stop them. They were too heavy for one kite.

Franz grabbed her arm and shook his head. "Today you learn the power of the love of Soman." With that said, Franz jumped off the edge of the cliff, pulling Raven and the kite with him.

Raven looked off to her right as Redd and John soon followed. She held her breath, waiting for the kite to free fall because it was bound to so much weight, but, to her surprise, it shot high in the air.

Franz tugged at her leg from below and pointed to where they were going. Raven looked ahead as they circled back toward the cliff. She banked hard, missing rock by only inches. She then heard from below, "You must open your heart and focus your mind on the great bear, and his power will flow through you like the wind." At that moment, she felt the kite surge forward at an ever increasing speed. Franz let out a yowl as they sped past John.

Raven pulled back on the kite, but Franz kept singing, driving the kite into a full loop. Franz looked up. "Stop trying to fight it. It's like jumping in the treetops."

It was wind that first filled her mind. Its roar bellowed loud and hard until all else was drowned out in a deafening white noise. It was through that noise that a form began to emerge from behind the mist of memory. It was then that a picture of the bear filled her mind. It was from many years back, when she had jumped off the mountain. It was the bear that had pulled them back up. Even on the cliff of ashes, he was there. Years earlier, it was he who had led the young children one by one to the temple. Years earlier, she saw him consoling her after her parents died. She had felt him then but did not know his name. Their lives had been woven together from the beginning, but she had never seen it for what it was. She had never stepped back far enough to see the tapestry that was her life. Deep within the pattern, she found what Franz had called her toward. Her heart overflowed with a warmth that has no name. She gripped the kite tighter as she began to sing. The kite soared high into the sky and then dove at a speed that pulled Franz's curly hair straight. She pulled up hard just over the water, with Franz's feet leaving a rooster tail of water behind them. She looked below at Franz with his hands stretched out to feel the spray of the water. She then noticed that he was no longer singing. She had driven the kite on her own. She sang the praise of the bear, remembering her life anew, and the kite flew faster. Just before she pulled up, she saw a paw come out of the water and slap Franz's outstretched palm. As they rose up the wall of the far cliff, she looked down and saw the great bear lying on his back, swirling in the tormented waters below. He waved at her and then quickly disappeared into the water.

They landed a little hard on the far cliff, sending Franz into a somersault. Franz bounced up out of a roll and ran toward Raven to give her a hug. She began to cry and asked, "What was that?"

Franz smiled. "It is what you have always held in your heart. We just set it free today."

Redd ran over and hugged Raven. "You were wonderful. Can you believe how we flew?"

"I felt like I was part of the wind." Raven gave Redd a kiss and looked out over the cliff. "I felt like I was free."

"Our traveler friends have a deep understanding of the great bear." Redd smiled as he looked back over the cliff. "It's like being in a different world."

Off in the distance, Max was waving Raven and Redd to join them as they made their way across the second island. In several hours, they had crossed the second island and were staring at the cliffs separating them from the villagers' island.

Raven strapped on her kite and looked for Franz, but he had already tied on to the villager that had taken him over days before. He tipped his knife to his eyebrow as if to say, "You can do this on your own." He then ran off the edge of the cliff with the villager close behind with the kite. Raven raced to the cliff's edge with her kite and launched into the air. Again the wind filled her mind with its deafening roar. The tapestry of her life played out before her, and there she saw the pattern of the weaver. Her heart sang out, free from the gloom of years past. As the heavy chains of remorse and guilt and pain fell away from her heart, the kite shot forward, racing the very wind that filled her mind. Time itself fell away as she swirled through the air. She was no longer tied to the cares that defined yesteryear; all that mattered now was the chase—the chase of her heart's desire. He filled her heart with warmth, and the kite soared.

Without knowing it, she had landed. She looked at the other as if to ask whether they had seen what she had seen, but they just talked among themselves as if it were just another flight. It was through the corner of her eye she saw Franz smile at her and wink, and then he was gone, bounding off after John toward Raven's old cabin.

That night, over a fire, Raven told her friends of her experience, and they shared in her joy. She slept well that night. It was the first good sleep she had ever had.

CHAPTER 33

MENDING A HEAVY HEART

EARLY THE NEXT MORNING, Raven awoke to a beam of light pouring through the cabin window. A blanket of silence lay over those still sleeping. Particles of dust danced through the light, moving like sparkles on shimmering water. Her mind was clear. As if in a trance, she focused in on one particle of dust making its way through the room. At first it seemed to bounce randomly, but as she lost herself in the particle she began to feel a rhythm to the movement. In the deeper parts of her mind, a melody began to accompany the dust particle. It started slow and simple but with time picked up tempo. The other dust particles that at first seemed to be unrelated now were all following the song that played in the recess of her mind. Redd rolled over and grabbed her hand. The sense of the song dimmed but did not fully dissolve. She looked over to Redd and smiled. A tear filled her eye. She had a week left, according to the man in the forest. She looked down at her hands, not sure whether yesterday was real or a dream. It was only a week ago that she had been ready to die. She stretched her fingers and felt the strength that had been given her. The rest of the cabin began to awaken, and the moment of silence was gone. Raven looked over at the small pack she would take with her. She would travel light. Once she had made ready, she stepped outside and found John near the forest's edge, staring into the trees.

John looked over to Raven, smiled, and then looked back at the forest. "You have heard the song of the bear. I can see it in your eyes."

Raven again became aware of the light rhythm of the song that danced on the very fringe of her consciousness. "I heard it in the silence of the cabin. What is it?"

"When I first learned to listen, I would need to concentrate on something very small. It was Soman himself that showed me the effect of his song." John waved his hand over the forest. "All of this is the effect of the song flowing like a river. The trees in front of us do not exist on their own. They are drawn into existence moment by moment through the song. They are the manifestation of the song in our world."

Raven looked up at John with a question on her face. "You mean they are not real?"

John bent down and picked up a twig on the ground with a leaf still attached. A mild breeze danced with the leaf in his hand. "Concentrate only on the leaf. In your mind, you will start to hear the song get more distinct."

Raven looked down at the leaf and saw it flicker in the wind. Several minutes later, she began to feel silly for staring at the leaf. But in the back of her mind, the rhythm of the leaf in the wind began to match a melody that was everywhere and yet nowhere. The longer she stared at only the leaf, the more distinct the melody became.

"It is always playing, the song of the bear. We have just learned not to hear it." John then moved the leaf across Raven's face. "Now see the leaf reforming itself through the song as it moves through the air."

Raven followed the leaf closely with her eyes. At first all she saw was the leaf, but then she gradually noticed that the leaf itself was not moving through the air as she had thought. The leaf disintegrated and reintegrated moment by moment as it moved like a ripple spreading across the water.

"You are now seeing what is real. Since birth your mind has been bent toward seeing things as permanent—moving along as if they were part of a large machine. If we ignore the song, all we are left with is the machine … but it is not real. It exists only in our minds. The song is what is real. It is what makes you real." John took Raven's hand and brought it up to her face.

Raven saw her hand and then, like the leaf, it began to break down and build up moment by moment. Gasping, she pulled her hand back. "I am like the leaf?"

"The part of you that we can see and touch is like the leaf." John then pointed to her forehead. "The part of you that is talking to me is special. It is more like the singer than the song ... but not quite either. You are a fusion of song and not-quite-song."

Raven spent a moment studying her hand with the song now clearly playing in her mind.

"Now I don't need to concentrate to hear and see it. It's all that I see. I used to think that the narrow path that we take in the forest stopped at the trees' edge ... but I was wrong. We are always on the narrow path. The song directs anyone who will listen to move in harmony with it. The piece of us that isn't the song must still choose to move in harmony with it, but over time you learn that it's crazy to move outside of the harmony." John looked down at Raven. "You saw the great bear while you were flying. You felt him in your heart. There is no greater joy. Over time, it is all your heart seeks. When you are on the path, you will be presented with many choices in the moment. You will not see where your choice will take you. All that you will know is that you are obeying an unheard command to maintain within the harmony of the song. But it is only within the harmony of the song that you feel the joy of being with Soman. Over time it is all that you will desire. At that point, to stray outside of the harmony is unthinkable. It would take you outside of the joy."

Raven looked up at John with a tear in her eye. "I'm going to die soon."

John smiled, reached down, and wiped away the tear. "I know. I could sense it in the song. My time is also short. I can feel it. There are many things in this life that I will miss ... most of all my family." John wiped a tear from his own eye and then reached around Raven's shoulder and gave her a hug. "But death isn't the end of the path; it is only one of many adventures we are given to strengthen us and bring us closer to Soman." John looked up at the sun and the blue sky. He then turned to Raven. "Do you still hear the song strongly in your heart?"

Raven was silent.

John walked toward the trees, and they split to form a path for his feet. "Follow me for a morning run." John increased his pace to a jog, and Raven followed closely behind. "Feel the sun on your face and let the joy of being in harmony with the bear fill your heart." John bounded forward at a pace that should not have been possible for a man his size.

Raven sped forward. As she looked at the trees to her left and right, she no longer saw static pillars of wood but instead saw the song of the bear flowing through the forest, creating and recreating moment by moment all that was around her. Soon she was lost in the song. Her legs pumped hard as she ran like the wind to keep pace with John. The sun beat down on her face. She felt her heart overtaken by joy. They suddenly emerged out of the forest not far from where they entered.

Raven bent over to catch her breath. "I could feel it. I could see and hear it."

John picked up his halberd, which he had left on the ground, and smiled. He turned to Raven and nodded. "It's time to get going."

CHAPTER 34

SHADOWS IN THE CHANNEL

IT TOOK ONLY SEVERAL hours to hike to the far side of the island. They left the villagers behind for this leg of the journey. Max and Mary looked over the cliff toward the fourth island. Max was strapped to Tracker, and Mary to Liney. They nodded to each other, and off the cliff they went. Max looked over to Mary, who was drifting thirty yards to his right. He tugged on Tracker's leg and then began to sing. The kite took off like a falcon on the hunt. They sped past Mary and Liney, nearly clipping their wing as they crossed over. Max smiled and waved. Now to his left he could see Mary shaking her fist at him and pulling on Liney with the other arm. Her kite shot forward, and the dance was on. Just as they had jumped from tree to tree when they were young, hunting in the forest, so now did they crisscross in the wind.

Max looked down at the churning water below. Through the middle of the channel he saw three massive shadows moving against the current. He motioned Tracker to dive lower for a look. Mary dove by to the right. Max waved his arm at the shadow, but Mary was not looking. Her kite continued its breakneck decline toward the rushing water below. The shadows in the water grew darker

Tracker looked down and nodded. Their kite dove after Mary, who did not look back.

Moments later, the channel filled with a rainbow of mist as the sea monsters below erupted from the turbulent waters. Max pulled his bow from his shoulder and steadied an arrow on his string. A beast as black as night erupted out of the waves below. Mary's kite diverted to the left, but they would not clear the gaping mouth of the beast. Max let the arrow fly. It found its target between the two eyes of the beast, creating a distant explosion of ash as it made a crater on impact. The beast moaned and tilted slightly but kept on target.

Then, from out of nowhere Raven's kite came shooting by from the side. She held out her long blade, which sang in the wind. The beast turned toward the sound but was too late. The long blade slashed across its ugly head, hissing as it separated flesh from flesh. Mary's kite flew just past the diverted head of the beast, clearing it by only inches. In order to miss the beast, the kite flew further down toward the water, which was now boiling from what lay beneath.

Two massive green eels suddenly broke through the surface. Their heads swayed high above the water like two cobras luring in their prey. Mary's kite flew just between them. Max could now see the sun glinting off the broadsword in her hand. Max let loose two more arrows, both of which found their marks on the foreheads of the beasts. Ash was still in the air as Mary's blade found its mark, slicing deep into the eel's neck. It moved through the thick flesh like a hot knife through butter. The eel's partner shot down toward Mary's kite but suddenly diverted right as Redd and John flew directly into its head. Redd stabbed with one hand while keeping the kite steady with his other. John, now standing on the beast's head, swung hard with the axe portion of his halberd as if he were splitting dark wood.

The beast ducked his head, and John was again hanging by the rope attached to Redd. The great black beast was now turning back toward the battle. Water hung in the air all around, and for a moment time seemed to stand still, imprinting the picture in Max's mind. He was brought out of his trance by Tracker yelling, "Sing!"

Max looked up and then remembered where he was. He began to sing, and their kite shot up toward the side wall of the fourth island. The rest of the kites were close behind. The three beasts below shot high in the air for one last chance at their prey but fell short. The kites landed hard on the ground.

Max cut loose his rope as soon as his kite hit the ground, and he ran toward Mary to scold her for diving down toward the water without looking. When he arrived, he saw Mary bent over, catching her breath. She stood up and looked at him. Max's heart melted as he grabbed her and hugged her tight.

Liney slapped them both on the back. "That was a little more excitement than I thought we would have this morning."

Redd unstrapped from his kite. "Those monsters were not there by accident."

John nodded.

Redd wiped the dark blood of the beasts off of his hooked spear. "Somehow they knew where we were going. They're protecting something."

Raven had an uneasy look on her face. "The fifth island is different from the rest." She looked back over the cliff with the rushing water below. The shadows were now gone. "It has an unprotected beach on the far side—the side where the cave with the stairs lies. The last time I was there gathering glow stones, I noticed footprints in the sand. They were not made by anything we have yet seen."

Redd slapped his spear on his other hand. "Those beasts have been trying to infiltrate onto our island for years. The only thing that stopped them was the rocks that protect the beach. Without protection from those things coming on land, that island could be crawling with beasts."

Mary was already at the forest's edge, looking in. "Then we had better hurry. Maybe we can get there before they are ready for us."

Max listened as she began to sing, and off they went into the woods.

CHAPTER 35

THE DARK POOL

They reached the final channel in less than an hour. Beneath the foam of the crashing waves, Raven could see nearly a hundred beasts slithering in the waters below. They were so tightly packed in that they had to constantly slide over the tops of each other to stay in motion. "So much for sneaking in unannounced."

"We don't need to fly low." Max pointed his hand up into the sky. "We can fly high above them."

Raven shook her head. "Near the end of the day we could do what you say. The winds will die down at that time. But at this time of the day, there's a strong downdraft on both sides. It drives the wind down with the current of the water. If we are to cross during the day, we must dive down low to catch the wind ... even with the song."

Redd looked across at the fifth island. "We can't wait till dark. That place will be crawling with creatures just like the water below."

Near the cliff's edge, Raven could hear the scrape of metal on metal. There stood Franz with a blade in each hand, running them over each other as he looked down into the water. He then looked back to Raven and tipped one blade to his eyebrow. Raven nodded and began to strap on her kite. She looked over to John with a worried expression on her face as if to ask whether this was where they would die.

John smiled but said nothing.

Raven tightened her straps and found an extra length of rope tied onto one wing. She looked over to Franz, who was tying himself in.

"A little extra rope can come in handy." He smiled briefly and then looked away as he tied himself up to the kite.

Raven was the only one to have ever flown this gap before. She set everyone at the side of the cliff. They would all launch together and stay close together to make as small a target as possible. With one wave of her hand, everyone launched.

Raven took the lead, diving straight down toward the water. She could see the beasts stirring below. With a burst of water that sounded like thunder, the water erupted with motion. Long necks and snake-like bodies rose out of the water like a forest being grown in a single moment. The monsters were packed so tightly together below that a man could have walked from one side of the channel to the other side without getting wet. The beasts had already risen above the level that the fliers would have to drop below to catch the fast wind. They were not going to make it. It was then that Raven felt a weight release from below. Moments turned to days as she watched Franz fall into the midst of the beasts. She looked at his harness, which had been cut by the blades he still clutched in his hands. His war cry was loud as he fell.

Raven followed him down, not wanting to leave him alone … even if they were all going to die. The others followed suit in a single-file line. Franz landed softly on the slanted neck of a beast and dug his knives in deep. As they found purchase, he slowed for a moment. It was then that Raven heard the faint hint of Franz singing the song that Mary had used to open the path. Franz bounded from one monster to the next, slashing as he went. The necks of the monsters spread like the trees of the forest, forming a path as he barreled through, singing at the top of his lungs. Raven followed him in on her kite, and the others were close behind. For a very long minute, they jetted through a surreal tunnel of green-and-black skin. None of the beasts' heads could penetrate into the path. Raven could feel the wind behind her. They were picking up speed. Looking beside her, she noticed the rope that Franz had tied to the kite. She smiled and let the rope down trail far below her. The sun was shining bright just ahead as the end of the path neared. Raven was still trailing Franz too far behind for him to grab the rope. It was then that a calm fell over her and her heart filled with the song. Her kite sped forward, and as Franz dove high in the air off of the last monster's back, he caught the rope as it went by him.

Raven pulled up hard, swinging Franz in a wide arc on the rope. The wind carried them high into the air, far above the beasts. Franz let out a war cry as he waved one knife in the air. The beasts below recoiled in unison, and Raven saw fear in their eyes. A moment later, the kites landed on an open plain on the fifth island.

The wind blew hard on the open field before them. Raven looked down at her kite and then let it go. The wind took it high in the sky. Redd bolted after it, but she called him back. She had been through so much with her kite. It was like a friend. The short path that she had left on this world would not bring her back here. It was better for her kite to be free, just as she now was. The wind blew hard, and it was not long before it was only a speck on the horizon. She smiled to think that perhaps in her journey after death she would see it again.

Raven turned to the sound of a rustling of the trees in the distance. Out of the forest, a yellow beast galloped straight for them. Max pulled down his bow and made ready an arrow, but Redd held his hand. "Your arrows will not work on that one."

Raven smiled as she recognized Charlie advancing. When Charlie arrived and bent down low for a back rub, the trees erupted with howls of disapproval from what sounded like a thousand beasts still hidden behind the forest's edge. The sound was deafening. Raven looked up at the sun, which was still high in the sky. There was no advantage to waiting. Their light would only get shorter as the day wore on. Redd mounted Charlie, holding his hooked spear out like a lance. Raven climbed up behind Redd and stood tall, her hair blowing hard in the wind. With one hand she took hold of Redd's collar, and with the other she unsheathed her sword and pointed forward. Charlie slowly began to trot back toward the trees from which he came. The others followed suit close behind. She looked down at John as if to ask if this was where they would die, but his eyes gave no answer. He only smiled and tapped his halberd on her sword.

Charlie was now galloping at full speed. His nostrils blew out smoke with every breath. Moments before they hit the edge of the forest, Raven again opened her heart to the will of the great bear and the trees spread before them into the narrow path. Charlie was running fast, and the trees were like a blur in the corners of Raven's eyes. Without warning, they burst into an opening filled with deformed beasts of dark blues and black. They were of every size, all with long fangs and red eyes that glowed in the dark of the forest. Redd was the first to draw blood with his spear. The beast howled as its side hissed into a crater of ash. A large beast with a head like a horn charged them from the side. Raven's sword twitched for a moment and then swung down hard, splitting the horn in two.

Charlie did not slow his pace. Up ahead was a beast the size of a barn with five red eyes and a mouth twice the size of Charlie. It raised its claws and howled like the thunder. From behind, Raven heard another howl and then felt a mild push on the back as Franz used her to springboard in a great arc toward the beast. Charlie dug his feet into the ground and breathed fire into the beast's body. Franz landed lightly high on the beast's chest. He swung up the body of the beast using his knives to gain purchase as he went. As he climbed, John and Mary ran straight into the beast, hacking at its legs. Ash and smoke filled the air with every blow. Raven looked up at the beast's head to find Franz standing square on its snout with his knives stretched out in front of its middle eye. He yelled his war cry and slashed across the eye. The beast toppled to one side as one leg gave way, leaving a clear path to the forest edge just behind. Charlie bounded for the trees. Raven opened the path, and the others followed close behind.

Raven looked back for Franz but did not see him. She bent down to Redd. "We need to go back. Franz is still back there." She pulled on his collar.

Redd shook his head. "The path only goes forward. We cannot go back. We must trust in the path."

Franz suddenly emerged through a tunnel of trees on the side wall of the path. He landed on Charlie's back just behind Raven. He looked up at her and tipped his blade to his eyebrow and smiled. Her heart glowed. She resolved never to doubt the path again. She looked back up at the rows of trees flying by.

They ran for an hour before the trees again opened up, this time to the island's dark gray beach and the sea beyond. There were no beasts in sight. Raven looked the beach over. She knew this place. The narrow path had led them close to the mouth of the cave where she had gathered the glow rocks so many years ago. It was there that she had seen the stairs like those near the top of the smoking mountain ... and the footprints of the beasts. Redd looked back at her for directions. Raven pointed to the jagged cliffs to her right.

Charlie moved slowly now toward the cliffs, looking from side to side. The others followed close behind. Raven had the sense that she was being herded into a trap, but there was no other way. Charlie blew fire at the trees to his right. The only sound they heard was the crackle of leaves burning and the hypnotic grate of the waves pulling away from the shore.

The tide was low, and they were able to walk around the first bend of the towering rocks before them without going into the sea. As they turned the corner, they came upon a hollow in the shadows of the cliff. Raven pointed her sword toward the spot. As they entered, there was a eary silence. At first they walked on sand and loose rubble, but farther in they found a wet floor glistening with the dim green of the rocks that glowed all around them. The warmth of the sun was now fully gone. On the far side of the flat landing was an opening that led down. Raven pointed there.

When they reached the far end, they found a wide set of stairs leading down into the rock. Raven could not tell if the rocks now glowed brighter or if her eyes had just adjusted to the darkness. The ceiling to the stairs was too low to ride Charlie in, so they dismounted. One by one, they slowly descended the black stairs. Behind, Raven heard the screech of metal as Franz ran his blade across the glowing green rocks. It did not penetrate. He nodded to John, who was now holding his halberd with both hands. They went deep into the earth until at last the stairs stopped and they found themselves in a circular domed room with a pool of water in the middle. The room glowed green, and the water was still like a mirror.

Raven looked around, but there was no way out except the way they came in. Behind them on the stairs above they could now hear the scratch of claws slowly descending the stairs. Charlie turned toward the stairs and blew a stream of fire up the tunnel. The walls echoed with the howls of beasts.

Raven again surveyed the domed room. "This is a trap. There is no way out." She then stepped over the pool and looked in. It was dark. All she saw was her reflection looking back at her.

John then walked to the pool. "This is where the path has led us, and this is where we must go." He then lowered his halberd into the water.

At first nothing happened. John began to withdraw the halberd but then stopped. A slow whirlpool began to form. Around the rock edges of the pool, a circular current flowed, faster and faster. Behind them the beasts again howled. The scratching on the stairs was getting louder. Raven looked down at the pool, which was now a swirling vortex with its center descending into the darkness that lay beyond. As they watched, the water spread to the sides. The bottom of the water, if there was a bottom, could no longer be seen.

Franz looked over the edge. "It's like the tunnels that we use to pass through the earth from one dark tree to the next." He then stood up and jumped in without another word. John followed close behind. Mary and Max looked at one another, nodded, and jumped in. The animals howled louder. Redd led Charlie to the edge, but Charlie pushed back. He looked back at the stairs and then at the pool. With trembling feet, Charlie stepped to the edge and stretched out his snout as far as he could into the hole of swirling water. Redd looked at Raven and nodded. They both jumped onto Charlie's neck, tipping the balance. Just before they all fell in, an arrow shot past Raven's ear. She looked toward the stairs and saw a creature painted in white, red, and black who had the head of a lizard with the torso of a man. Below, his body was fused with a lizard like Charlie. Its only clothing was a dark breastplate with the image of a dragon emblazoned in the center with green glow rocks. Its face was filled with anger. As Raven fell into the hole with Redd and Charlie, she saw the dark creature point its finger at her. Their eyes met, and she understood that they would meet again.

Looking back up to where the entrance of the hole should have been, she saw only darkness. They tumbled through the dark tunnel and popped out the other side. They sat with the rest of the party in a domed room identical to the one they had just been in. Raven looked over to the stairs, half expecting to see the warrior emerge, but she did not. There was no one waiting for them. She looked at Redd and said, "I guess they didn't think we'd ever make it into the water." Raven looked back at the hole from which they had come. It had filled back up with water and was now perfectly still.

John was already walking up the stairs in front of them. Raven and Redd climbed onto Charlie, and they all began to make their way up. As they climbed, Raven ran her hand across the side walls of the stair. They were made of a smooth blue stone studded with the green glow stones. She knew that blue stone. It could be found only on the fourth island. Somehow that water tunnel had carried them back across the channel. The stairs then opened up into a massive underground opening. Before them lay the remnants of a massive underground city. All the buildings were hewn from the same blue rock in the tunnel. Massive stalactites of the glowing green rock hung from the top of the cave, giving the sense of twilight.

Some of the buildings were still standing, but many had been toppled over. Rubble lay in the streets, giving the impression that a great battle had been fought here. On the buildings that still stood, there were claw marks an arm's length deep. The city was deathly quiet except for the sound of trickling water that ran in a channeled river through the middle of the city. The party followed a road that ran on the side of the river.

Redd looked back at Raven. "This place is old. Do you remember ever hearing of such a place on the island?"

Raven shook her head. "The closest thing would be stories that we told young children of an ancient people of the sea that had built a fantastic city out of gold and gems. It was just a fairy tale. I don't know of anyone that took it seriously."

Redd nodded. "What happened to those people in the fairy tale?"

"There was some cataclysmic event, and their city sunk into the sea ... there may have also been something about a dragon." Raven shrugged. "Typical fairy tale."

Charlie stopped next to John, who paused to look at a stone plaque near the river's edge. John ran his finger across the picture on the stone. "This is a map of the city." He looked around him and pointed to a large stalactite above and then an engraved one on the rock. He then pointed to a spot on the map. "We are here." He followed his finger down the river to the cave's edge. "This road seems to take us to the far end of the city." He followed his finger back to the area where they came up the stairs. It was marked with a small red stone.

Max pointed his bow at the far edge of the map on the other side. There, near the end of the river, was another red stone. "If Raven is right, and we are under the fourth island … then this red dot should get us to the third island."

Everyone nodded and picked up the pace. Raven looked over at a statue of a mother and child walking near the river's edge. They were adorned with robes studded with jewels. Under the robes were the hind feet of panthers. Raven thought little of it. In front of them on a leash was a lizard like Charlie, only much smaller. She lowered her sword to the street and picked up a necklace with a small lizard made of glow rock tied on it. "It must have belonged to a child." Raven looked around her. "If there was a battle here … where did all the people go? There is only fallen rock. There are no fallen bodies."

Max took his bow off his shoulder and nodded. "Something is not right here."

The road ended abruptly at the sidewall of the cave. The river ran through a tunnel to their right. To their left was a small road that led along the cave's wall to a set of stairs. Once they were at the bottom of the stairs, they found another familiar domed room with a pool of water in the center. This time Redd dipped his spear into the water, and again it began to twirl. As they waited for the hole to appear, they looked at each other in silence. Raven knew what everyone was thinking and needed to say nothing. Something terrible had happened to that city.

The water in the pool receded into the darkness below. One by one, they jumped in. As the darkness enveloped Raven, she brushed her hand in front of her eyes. She could see nothing. Soon they landed in another domed room with a set of stairs leading up. Redd and Raven led Charlie up the stairs with sword at hand and spear ready. The path was lit by the green stones as before, but now set in a background of yellow metal, although Raven could not be sure of the color. In the green light, everything looked different.

When they reached the top of the stairs, they again saw a river running through a massive underground opening. This time there was no city. The only structure sitting on the smooth gold floor was a single pyramid with steps going up on all three sides. The pyramid stretched up high toward the cave's roof. At its base sat a solid black cube one third the height of the pyramid. Raven reached down to a bracelet that was handed down to her from her grandmother. She unlatched it and walked over to one of the brighter stones on the wall. There in the middle of the bracelet was a pyramid with a cube in front.

She looked over to Redd. "This bracelet has been in my family for many generations." She pointed to the pyramid on her bracelet. "This is the same object here in the cave. This bracelet came from here. *We* may have come from here."

John was over by the river, motioning them to come along. Raven jumped onto Charlie and spurred him on in the opposite direction. They raced across the vast gold floor toward the pyramid that lay at its center. When she arrived, she saw that it was much larger than it seemed from a distance. Charlie led her to one of the staircases that led to the top. On either side of the stairs stood two rows of statues, lining the stairs all the way up. Without hesitation, she jumped off Charlie and began climbing the stairs. As she sped up the staircase, she passed hundreds of statues her size or larger of people from this lost culture. At first she paid little attention to them, but the farther up she went, the more her eyes hung upon their forms.

The statues near the base were of people that had a normal look to them. They were dressed simply and relatively unadorned. As she rose, the statues became increasingly strange. Men were adorned as women, and women as men. They wore strange clothing, with the heads and claws of animals as hats and draping dresses. Farther up, most of the statues seemed to wear masks of animals, although something was not quite right. As she passed into the middle third of the pyramid, she could sense a definite shift in the statues. The clothing had become very subtle, if there was clothing at all. The form of the people themselves began to have a more animalistic appearance. Some were hunched over, and others had limbs that seemed too long for their bodies. Their faces, though, were the most disturbing. At first she thought they were wearing masks as those below them were, but she came to believe that the animalistic faces she saw were real. Near the top, the statues only partially represented what she would consider human, with animal heads on human bodies, and various animal parts seamlessly fused onto human torsos. She was nearly to the top when she stopped and stared into the face of one of the statues. It had a fully human torso that was fused to the body of a lizard like Charlie. It was the thing she had seen on the fifth island. The vulgar reality that the bizarre statues she had seen on the way up were not a product of imagination but instead representations of real creatures washed over her like a wave. Variations of the half-person, half-lizard lined the remaining climb, their lizard faces looking up the stairs. The top of the pyramid flattened off. There in the middle was a pedestal. Deep claw marks ran across the floor. On top of the pedestal lay only a base of twisted metal with teeth marks around it. Something had bitten off the top statue. She looked down at the golden floor far below. She could make out her friends in the distance, making their way along the river.

She had seen enough. She took off her ankle bracelet and left it near the ripped-out statue. Whatever her ties were with this ancient culture, they would end today. She wanted nothing to do with this page in history. She bounded down the stairs and jumped onto Charlie, who was waiting for her at the bottom. Together they sped toward the others, who had almost reached the far end of the cave.

As they turned toward the stairs that now lay before them, John paused and looked over to Raven. "Did you find what you were looking for on the gold mountain?"

"Hints of the past. Nothing more."

John nodded and looked away. With his halberd in hand, he bounded down the stairs to the next domed room. This time Mary dipped her sword in the water and the water began to swirl.

As they waited for the tunnel to appear, Redd looked over to Raven. "So what did you see on the golden mountain?"

"I saw many things that should not be. We will need to be careful. There are things that have lived in this cave that you could not have dreamed of. They are waiting somewhere."

John was the first to go into the tunnel this time. Raven was the last.

CHAPTER 36

THE DARK CITY

WHEN RAVEN POPPED OUT of the hole, she was met with the smell of freshly spilled blood. Four of the lizard men lay hewn on the floor around the pool. Mary looked back at Raven while she washed the blood from her sword in the swirling water of the pool. John was leaning against the wall that led to the stairs. When he turned toward them, she saw four arrows embedded in his breastplate and one in his shoulder. He ran his halberd sideways across the four arrows, breaking them off. "They just embedded in the armor." He pointed down at the emblem of the bear on the breastplate and smiled. "It's not the first time he saved me." John then looked down at the arrow sticking out of his shoulder.

Raven watched as Mary pulled his shirt away from the wound and looked at Max. Max picked up one of the stray arrows, examined it, and nodded. Mary turned back to John, braced herself, and pulled the arrow out. It came out clean but left a dark hue around the entry site.

Redd took the arrow and showed it to Raven. "Poisoned with the venom of the sea beasts."

Raven looked up at John, who was now moving his shoulder around. "It doesn't feel that bad." John smiled and patted Redd on the back.

Raven glanced at Redd with an uneasy look and then peered up the stairs. There were several blood trails leading up. "They meant to finish this here. There are probably more at the top. We will need a plan."

Mary tapped her sword on Raven's and pointed toward Charlie.

Moments later, Mary and Raven came barreling up the stairs on Charlie's tail. They held tight to a rope with one hand and their swords in the other. When they hit the open cave, arrows flew from all directions. Those aimed at Charlie bounced off his heavy scales. As for Mary and Raven, no arrow touched them as their swords hummed picking off each approaching arrow in flight. Raven saw at least twenty of the lizard men circling around them. Charlie let out a burst of fire, charring two as they stood there. Mary and Raven attacked straight forward with the others now behind them.

Raven's blade sang as it slew one monster after another. She then felt a heavy blow to her side. The tail of one of the beasts landed hard on her ribs. The beast turned, faced her, and pointed a finger at her. It lifted its head up to the sky, and fire erupted from its mouth. In its hand it carried a massive maul. It swung it high in the air, meaning to crush Raven in one blow as Redd's spear pierced it in the chest. Its entire torso turned to ash.

Raven looked back at what was left of the lizard men. Charlie blew streams of angry fire at each one that lay dead, reducing them to ash.

Raven looked around at the city of the second isle as she dipped her sword into the river to clean it. It was very different from the first city they had passed through. Its buildings slanted and curved as if to defy any pattern or resemblance to nature. As they walked along the river road, she stared at the many pieces of sculpture along their path. Unlike before, there were no edifices bearing the likenesses of people or creatures. Shapes of warped and twisted metal erupted from the black road. They seemed to reach out to the heavens in agony. Unlike the first city, there was no rubble in the streets. It was eerily clean. But again there was no sign of any people. It took an hour to reach the other side. To their left was a small road to the next water tunnel. In front of the opening to the stairs lay a high pile of large stones.

It was then that Raven saw the city come alive like a slithering den of snakes. Lizard men crept out of holes in the buildings, scaling down to the streets.

"There are hundreds of them." Redd looked around him and shook his head. He then looked to the river. "Hand me that rope." He pointed to Franz, who pulled a length of rope hanging from his waist.

Redd tied the rope tight around Charlie's neck and then wrapped each one of them to the rope in single file. The lizard men were now advancing quickly, with arrows bouncing off the ground beside them and careening into the river beyond. The lizard men stopped as they encircled the party up against the river's edge. Mary and Raven pulled out their swords, which were now humming in anticipation. One of the lizard men made a loud grunting noise, and they burst toward the group. It was then that Redd gave a hard slap to Charlie's backside. Charlie dove into the river and was swept away. One by one, each of the party flew into the river. Raven heard Franz's war cry behind her.

CHAPTER 37

DRAGON BONES

JOHN LOOKED AROUND HIM in the rushing water of the river. They moved past dark rocks and then shot into an open body of water. Above he could see the light of the sun and swirling waves. They were passing under the current of the last channel. He could still feel the pull of the river's current as it pulled them along. Ahead he could see a hole in the wall with darkness beyond. Before he could decide whether that was where he wanted to go, he was swept into darkness. Ahead he could make out a red glow. His lungs now burned for air. As his mind began to fade, he felt the rope tighten, and suddenly he was thrown out of the water and onto a golden rock on the water's edge. He slowly lifted his head to see Charlie dug in tight to a rock upstream, and Redd, with the hook of his spear, was dug into the rock just behind. He looked behind him to see each of his party fly out of the water as the rope tightened on each one of them.

As he rose, his eyes were drawn to the walls of the great opening. For as far as he could see, the walls shimmered with gold. Embedded in the shiny walls were large crystals that glowed red. Peppered throughout were what looked like small embedded stones. Across the river lay a mountain of dark red scales that began to unfold before his eyes.

"I have been watching you for a long time, John." Xaphan's horned head uncoiled out from his twisted body, his neck now stretching high into the air. "Do you know how long it took to create those überlizards you killed? Some of those parts are hard to come by, John."

Xaphan ran one of his claws down a golden necklace. Hundreds of heavy gold beads hung around his neck. As John's eyes cleared, he perceived that the beads in the necklace were gold-covered skulls—human skulls. John looked back at the golden walls and could now see that there were skulls embedded in the gold.

Xaphan smiled. "Like what I've done with the place?" His front leg waved across the vast golden hall. "One does what one can with what one has lying around." His claw then returned to the necklace, clicking down the string of skulls one at a time. "I used to use them as part of my creations, but in the end they proved to be bothersome—never fully appreciative of my artistic prowess."

Xaphan's claw then stretched out to John. John held his halberd high, but the dragon's claw moved slowly, and John held still. The claw then scratched against the emblem of the bear on John's breastplate. "Over time it became personal." He continued to scratch against the emblem, deforming the image. "It was said that men were made in his image to represent his glory. They came to be a symbol of him to me. The one you know as the bear. He banished us from the higher places to scratch out an existence in this 'reality.'"

Xaphan raised both of his forelegs high in the sky, waving them about as he rolled his eyes. His claw then went back to his necklace, clicking down one skull at a time. "But his reality is not my reality. That was at the core of our initial disagreement that led us to revolt. I have the right to create my reality as I see fit. I will not be restrained by his forms of creation. In fact, I take great joy in rearranging his creations as I see fit." His claw continued down the long string of skulls. "I especially enjoy rearranging those who were meant to bear his image. It reminds me that I am in full control—that I am the master of my chosen reality." He then pointed his claw at John. "You know what it is to create your own reality, don't you, John? That mechanical house that you put together not so long ago. Crude to be sure, but nevertheless an obvious attempt to create your own reality."

John stood tall with his halberd at his side. "I gave that up. I am in the service of Soman now." He looked over at Mary, Max, and Franz, who stood by the bank of the river and watched on.

Smoke puffed out of Xaphan's nostrils. "A slave to his reality, you mean!"

"My heart is now free to follow its desire, and that desire is to follow whatever path Soman sets before me. I am on that very path right now."

Xaphan turned his head away from John and held it high. "How is that shoulder feeling, John ... getting a little cool?"

John rubbed his shoulder, which was feeling cold, looked up, and smiled. "Never felt better."

"Yessss, of course. That arrow that pierced your shoulder was dipped in a poison I made myself. Poison is somewhat of a specialty of mine. It is a thousand times more potent that the poison that is still festering in Raven." Xaphan waved to Raven. "Don't worry, Raven; I have not forgotten you. Welcome home. Thank you for returning that ankle bracelet that your ancestor stole from me." Xaphan toyed with a small piece of gold in his other hand and then threw it into a massive pile of gold jewelry.

Raven shook her fist. "You will die today."

A broad smile crept across the dragon's face. "All in good time, my dear ... all in good time." Xaphan then scratched under his chin as if lost in thought. "Oh yes ... John and the poison ... you will be dead before the end of the day, John. How does that make you feel? Like you said yourself, John, you are on the path the bear set for you. His path has led to death, John. He left you here to die."

John looked over his shoulder down the great golden hall. There in the distance he saw the black tree filled with flame.

Xaphan ran a claw across the rock floor beneath him as if drawing something and looked away. "Loyal to the last, I see. Not that it makes a difference to me anyway. You will all die ... loyal or not."

John stood silent for a moment. Raven was now standing right next to him. He felt a sense of calmness wash over himself. In a calm, low voice, John said, "You won't stop us from destroying that tree."

Xaphan roared with laughter. "Stop you? Why would I do that? If all I wanted was your death you would be dead already. It has been some time since I have had some decent entertainment. The black tree can take care of itself. Now get along, John." Xaphan waved his claw away from them as if to send them on their way. "Finish out your short, pointless, unimaginative life as you see fit. I will collect the skulls when the tree is done with you. My halls were in need of some new decoration."

John turned without saying a word and began walking toward the black tree.

Mary ran up to John as he walked. "Don't believe a word that dragon says, John. Soman will always be with you. He will save you."

John patted Mary on the back and pulled her to his side as they walked. "He already has. But that doesn't mean I won't die."

Mary looked up at John with shock on her face.

John smiled. "All paths eventually lead us through death, Mary. It is not for us to choose our death in this world. We are called to follow the path with joy in our hearts. What happens on the path is the business of Soman. My only choice is that of whether to stay on the path. And right now that black tree is right in the middle of my path." John picked up his pace, and the others followed close behind.

CHAPTER 38

THE TREE OF FIRE

As THEY DREW NEAR to the burning black tree, they began to feel the heat of its flames. From afar it looked like the tree was motionless, but that illusion was lost as they approached. John watched as the burning limbs writhed around and over each other, creating tangles of dark wood that would perpetually tie and untie themselves. The pattern was never the same. And through the openings flew hundreds of flaming silver birds with long, jagged beaks. It was wondrous to watch as limb and bird danced in the flame. Occasionally John could catch a glimpse of the massive tree's trunk though the fiery mesh.

John heard a faint *tink* to his side. A dark arrow slid across the golden floor and came to rest in front of him. John looked around his shoulder to a hundred of the lizard men crawling out of the river and making their way toward them. Five more arrows landed short and slid by him on the smooth floor. John looked back toward the burning tree. Even though it was still a hundred yards away, the heat was stifling. He did not understand how they would be able to even get close to it, much less penetrate its writhing branches. John looked back at the lizard men ... they were fast approaching.

"We need to head for the tree. It's our only chance!" John motioned everyone to follow him. As they ran, he suddenly felt a cool breeze to his side. To his right he could see a dark opening in the cave wall. The fresh air was coming from there. It then occurred to him that the burning tree was much like a forge, and this was the breeze that stoked it. John veered left, staying in the cool breeze as they headed straight for the tree.

Mary and Max were now running hard at his side. To his left, Redd and Raven were riding Charlie with Franz riding his tail, sitting backward, raising his knives to the sky at the lizard men who were hot in pursuit.

Mary turned to John. "How can we get through that?"

John did not know. "We just keep running the path, Mary. We don't have to figure out how we get through. Soman has already planned for that. We just need to stay true to the path." John looked behind him. The lizard men were nearly upon them when the bearded man from the forest jumped out of a shadow in the cave's wall. He raised his sword and slew the first three lizard men.

John looked straight ahead. "Everyone behind me." Without breaking stride, John ran straight into the mesh of fiery limbs. A moment before he made contact, the branches separated into the narrow path. The cool breeze followed them through a tunnel of fire and dark limbs. John ran with his eyes wide open, not sure he believed what was happening in the moment. Behind him he heard the croaks of lizard men near the mouth of the tunnel. In that surreal moment, John's mind paused on the fact that the path was not closing behind. He had not seen that before. Through the tunnel of fire, John could see Xaphan raise his head, smoke rolling from his nostrils.

"Tanner ... you are like an itch I have been dying to scratch for years." Xaphan whistled, and the lizard men stopped in their tracks. They then slowly turned in toward Tanner, who held his sword high.

"Don't you ever wash your pets, Xaphan? They smell worse than that foul beast of yours I cut the heart out of when we first met."

Xaphan raised his head to the ceiling, and fire spewed forth from his mouth, licking the golden hall with red and orange flame. He then opened his wings and flew into the midst of the lizard men, who had now formed a circle around Tanner. "If it is any consolation, Tanner, I can assure you that you will leave no such odor."

As Xaphan took a deep breath, Tanner charged the ring of lizard men, killing ten before the dragon fire consumed him and thirty of the lizard men nearby. Xaphan kicked the charred skeleton of one of the lizard men. "An acceptable sacrifice, I suppose." He then turned toward the remaining lizard men, who now watched his every move. He pointed one claw toward the opening through the flaming branches of the tree. Without hesitation, the lizard men picked up their chase and headed into the black tree's inferno.

John saw Redd reaching out his hand toward Tanner through the long tunnel and let out a howl of anger.

The dragon men advanced quickly through the fire tunnel. They were nearly a hundred yards into the tunnel when John heard an enormous crunching sound. Howls and moans filled the fiery tunnel as the narrow path now closed fast behind with a vengeance. Fiery limbs wrapped around the lizard men as the path closed, crushing them in midstride—but that was not the worst of it. The silver birds were now emerging from one side of the tunnel in full flight and reemerging into the other sidewall. They were like arrows with wings, piercing straight through the lizard men as if they were not even there.

John emerged from the path under the canopy of the black tree. Everyone piled out just before the path closed. The cries of the lizard men suddenly fell silent as the tree closed behind, leaving only the sound of crackling wood burning. The breeze still blew through the branches of the tree but was much warmer now.

Max nudged his elbow into John's side and pointed up. John followed the massive trunk up to the apex of the canopy. There at the top were thousands of the silver birds, lining the limbs of the tree so thickly that no black could be seen. As the waves of heat passed over the canopy, they made the tree look as if it were plated with silver, shimmering in the light of the fire all around. John nodded and put his finger to his lips, asking for silence.

Without a word, the party slowly moved across the golden floor, which glowed red from the reflection of the fire above. They were careful to stay in the path of the breeze that blew behind them. Eventually they reached the massive trunk of the dark tree. Raven reached out to touch the bark, but Franz grabbed her hand and pulled it away. He signaled her not to touch any of the bark, making a funny face as if he were melting.

John looked up at the silvery ceiling. He knew what was coming once they laid an ax to the tree. He signaled to the others what they were to do. When everyone understood, he positioned Mary and Raven next to each other and outlined a large circle on the trunk of the tree. John watched as Mary and Raven sunk their blades deep into the wood. The blades cut through the wood like hot knives through butter. The tree shivered as it was pierced, and the whole canopy seemed to come alive.

Mary and Raven quickly cut a deep cone into the trunk. It was tall enough for Charlie to pass through but was only several feet deep. John stepped into the shallow hole and began to hack away at the inner wood, slicing off large blocks of wood as he went. Mary and Raven worked beside him, cutting away at the wood, helping him create a tunnel in the tree.

John poked his head out of the tree and looked up above. The silver limbs had turned black, and the birds now flew in a great circle above, gaining speed. John watched as Max held his bow with an arrow at the ready. Franz stood at his side with no fear in his eyes. Max turned toward him. "We need to hurry, John. Time is running out."

Three birds separated from the flock above and now dove down toward the hole in the tree. Franz pointed toward the lead bird. Max nodded and pulled back his bow and let an arrow fly. He quickly reloaded, and soon three arrows found their mark in the breasts of the silver birds. They fell to the golden floor with a thud.

Franz leaned over and ran his blade across the neck of one of the birds. The blade easily sliced through. The head rolled to the side, resting where its eyes stared up at the boys. The red fire in its eyes slowly faded.

John looked back at the hole in the tree. It was now deep enough for Charlie to fit into the hollow. He whipped out huge blocks of wood with swipes of his tail. Redd was busy moving the blocks of wood from the back of the tunnel to where Charlie could swoosh them out. Massive chunks of wood flew from the hole in the tree and slid across the golden floor. Up above, the flock of silver birds shifted. They now dove in unison at the hole in the tree.

John backed into the hole. "Mary, come quick"

Mary wiped the sweat from her brow and turned to the opening of the tree. She held her blade high, and its metal hummed. "Here they come."

As the birds approached, the light from the surrounding fire dimmed under their shadow. They struck hard, as if they were a single spear being plunged into a man, but Mary's blade was up to the task. It swung high and low at lightning speed, not letting a single bird through the opening that Mary guarded. John went deeper in to help Raven cut away block after block of wood. Out of the corner of his eye, he could see Max and Franz helping Redd move the blocks of wood in front of Charlie's tail. Redd yelled, "Wood!" and Mary moved to the side as block after block of wood was ejected from the tree's center.

John turned to see the birds up above now, swarming like hornets. They fell from the sky like a rain of arrows. Franz brought a wedge-shaped piece of wood toward the cave's entrance and held up his hand. Redd and Max loaded a massive chunk of wood in front of Charlie's tail. Franz waited and then let his arm fall and yelled, "Wood!" Mary moved to the side, and the block of wood shot toward the wooden cave's entrance and then went airborne as it hit the wooden ramp. The boulder of wood shot high into the air. Many of the diving birds could not divert in time and sunk deep into the wood on impact. Others that were able to divert ran hard into the trunk of the tree, fully embedding themselves into the wood.

For hours John and Raven dug through the wood without rest. John looked over at Raven. "We need the tree to fall on the opposite side that we came in on so we can leave under the protection of the cool breeze. The tree will still be burning when it falls."

John pointed down at the rough wooden floor. "Follow the rings to the other side. I will meet you on the other end."

As John dug through the wood, he thought of how his life had flowed over the last years. His mind wandered from thoughts of his marriage to his wife's death and the bitter despair that had followed. His mind moved to the great bear and how he had guided him out of that despair and into a new life. Now, for the life of him, he could not imagine how it would be off the path that he was on. Hours later, he was brought back into the moment by the sound of Raven's blade bursting through the wood in front of him. She cut the block of wood and pulled it out to see John smiling at her. They had made it around the tree. John and Raven then hollowed out that side of the tree until they heard a great creaking noise.

John looked over at Raven, and then began to run for the opening. Mary called from the opening of the tree, "All the birds have gone. What's going on in there?"

John ran through the opening and waved for everyone to follow. Wood now burst out from the tree's base as it began to twist. The great tree groaned as it began to tilt to one side. Above it looked as if the very sky was falling. Straight ahead the burning branches began to lift up in the air as the tree fell. John and his group ran across the gold floor to the cave's edge along the line of the cool breeze. He did not look back as the tree hit the ground. The whole cave shook with the weight of the tree.

John was now at the side of the cave. He looked into the cave, where the fresh air had come from, but it led straight up. It was not the exit he had hoped for. Up above, the sky was now partially visible through the thick cloud of silver birds that swarmed madly above them. John looked back toward the river. It was the only way out, but they would never make that run without the birds seeing them. He rubbed his shoulder. It now had no warmth. He could no longer move the arm. He shifted his weight as he felt the weakness in the leg on that side. His time was growing short. It was then that he knew in his heart how this must end. He smiled and turned toward his friends. He hugged each one and whispered something into Redd's ear.

"Wait until the flock is diving, and then make haste along the side of the cave to the river and take it out." John smiled and looked out at the burning tree.

Franz pulled on John's coat with a tear in his eye. John smiled and knelt down. "I will be all right, Franz. Remember to stay strong and hold to the path."

Franz nodded, tears now filling his eyes.

John brushed Franz's tears away. "Do not fear death. It is only an entryway to another path. We will see each other soon enough."

With that John turned away and took off toward the opposite side of the cliff. Halfway across the golden floor, he began to shout and wave his halberd in the air. The flock of silver birds shuddered for a moment and then formed into a single diving formation and took aim at John. John was now running as fast as he could with a limp. His left leg now had little strength. To his side, he saw his friends making their way along the opposite edge of the cave. They were nearly halfway there when he heard a voice from across the river.

"It's not over, John. They are coming for you." Xaphan laughed as he watched from his perch, his forelegs lying contentedly on his belly. "How's that leg doing, John? Still happy with your path?"

John ran hard. He would not make the river. His friends were now at the river's edge, watching. John then stopped and turned toward the advancing spearhead of birds.

From afar Xaphan bellowed, "Mind the skull, John. It will not look good on my wall if it is crushed by one of the silver darts."

The cave filled with the laughter of Xaphan, but John did not hear it. His eye now followed the lead bird. An overwhelming peace overtook him, and he knelt down, pointing the spear of his halberd toward the oncoming storm of silver birds. With his last breath, he spoke only one word: "Beautiful." With that, the flock of birds ran him through, piercing his body a thousand times.

CHAPTER 39

JUDGMENT

XAPHAN SPREAD HIS WINGS and flew over to the spot where John had died. He moved the remains around with one of his claws, looking for something he could use. He stepped back, shook his head, took a deep breath, and blew a great cloud of fire over the remains. As the fire cleared, the great bear was standing on the spot with John's bones in his arms.

Xaphan stepped back. "I sensed your presence."

Soman looked up at the dragon with fire in his eyes. "How could you have not? I have seen the atrocities that you have committed with my creation. It is time for you to be held accountable for all you have done."

Xaphan looked away. "I choose to live in my own reality. In my world, your accountability means nothing."

The great bear then looked upon Xaphan. "You will accompany my servant John into the cave you have so longed to go to, and there you will find the nature of your reality."

With that Soman disappeared with the bones of John, and Xaphan found himself in his old angelic form, standing in front of the small cave with the spirit of John standing next to him.

* * * * *

John looked down upon himself, not sure what to think. The form of his body was intact and yet different. There beside him stood Xaphan in mannish form, standing several feet taller than John.

Xaphan looked down at the spirit of John. "Will we never be done with your tiresome face, John. Come with me. Whatever mischief your bear has in store for us, one thing I am certain of: you will not survive this in your paltry form. As for me, I'm still in control of the path I take. I have longed to explore this cave for years."

Xaphan led John deep into the cave. They went past a sharp curve and then came to a living area with sign of previous fires. Xaphan nodded. "So that's how he evaded my flame." He ran his hand over the charred rock just before the tight bend. Xaphan kicked what he found on the ground, and they walked on.

John looked about him and had no fear. The peace that had enveloped him before the birds struck still held tight over him. Farther down the cave, they came to a T intersection. To the left, a bright white light shone; to the right, there was only darkness. Xaphan looked down at John with contempt. "This is where your journey ends, John. What you see before you is the light of the Old One. I looked upon him years ago, but his light will consume a being such as you."

With that Xaphan walked on ahead into the tunnel of light. John waited where he was and listened as he heard what sounded like thunder. He then heard a language he did not recognize. Xaphan screamed, and then there was silence. John stood still for a moment, not knowing for sure what to do. He then felt a tingling in his heart that beckoned him to walk forward into the light.

As John's foot passed into the light, he felt pinpricks, as if he were shivering. The tunnel was long, and as he walked he noted that he was getting heavier and more hairy. John raised his hand to his face and saw what looked like a paw. Was this some form of judgment? The farther he went, the hairier he got. When he reached the edge of the cave, he looked out at two thrones. On the first was an image so bright he could not define it. To his right was a man of light that he recognized as Soman, even though he had never known him as a man. Resting across Soman's lap was a flaming sword. A voice from behind the light listed off the many sins of John's life as he stood and looked on. John waited for the punishment that he was sure to befall him, as it had Xaphan, but the flaming sword lay quiet on the lap of Soman. When the long litany of sins had been read, Soman set the sword to the side and opened his arms. "Well done, my good and faithful servant."

John then stepped into the light. It was only then that he noticed that he had taken on the form of a bear, like that of Soman. John now stood directly in front of the man of light. "How is this possible?"

Soman then took John's hand and let his finger fall through the hole in his own. "You are my friend, John. How could this be any other way?" With that Soman embraced John, and he returned to his mannish form.

CHAPTER 40

THE PATH CONTINUES

RAVEN HELD HER EYES wide open as the underground river swept her through the darkness. When they finally emerged from the tunnel, she looked down at the roots of the large island and saw the remnants of a vast stone city. Coral and sea plants now filled the streets. In one corner of the city, she saw a huge statue of a woman. For a moment she saw her own face in that cold, stony image. The river's current was now gone, and her lungs burned as she began swimming to the surface.

When she broke the surface of the water, she found the others being pulled into a small rowboat. A familiar face looked down upon her with a helping hand.

"Tom! How did you know to find us here?" Raven looked out at the island in the distance.

"Soman came to me last night and told me it was time to go fishing. I have been here all day." Tom pulled Raven up into the boat. "It looks like we are still missing one. Where is John?"

With that the whole boat burst into tears, and Raven recounted John's final stand in the golden cave. Tom wept as he listened. He then picked himself up and lifted up the gold ring. *Eros* was nearly upon them. The spear passed through the ring, and soon they were all on board.

* * * * *

Redd gripped the railing and ran his hands along it as if it were a long lost friend. The crew came and welcomed everyone. Redd then looked behind them and noticed a yellow splotch following them in the sea.

He ran to rear of the boat and saw Charlie swimming as hard as he could. Redd ran to a hatch to the lower level and opened the large door in the back of *Eros*. As he passed through the hold, he saw Raven's old kite lying against the side of the ship. He stopped for a moment as he recalled that kite blowing off into the horizon. He then came to his senses and remembered why he come down. Redd ran to the opening in the rear of *Eros* and waved Charlie on. The happy lizard picked up his pace and finally was able to get one claw onto wood. Once he had a grip, he pulled himself in and shook off the water. Redd hugged him and scratched him behind the ear.

Redd led Charlie up on deck, and the crew immediately went for their weapons. Redd held up his hand. "That won't be necessary, boys. This one's friendly. Aren't you, boy?" Redd tickled Charlie behind the ear, and he rolled over for a belly rub. Fire erupted from his nostrils and set a small sail on fire. Redd smiled and patted out the fire.

One by one, each of the men came and petted Charlie. It was not long before he was a part of the crew. That night was a quiet night.

CHAPTER 41

REMEMBERING

THAT NEXT MORNING, THEY found themselves out on the open sea. Raven woke up early and went out onto the deck, where she found Tom and Franz sitting on the back of the *Eros*, throwing fish heads at the sharks. Raven sat down next to Franz. He was quiet this morning.

Raven picked up a fish head out of the bucket and threw it into the water. "Did John talk to you much about the path after you die?"

Franz looked up at her and then looked back into the pail for another fish head. "He said the path didn't end at death ... that it just keeps going."

Raven raised her ankle to show Franz. The poison was returning. Her entire foot now was nearly black. "I think I will see him before you."

Franz looked up into Raven's eyes and gave her a hug. "He once told me that running the narrow path is sometimes like being squeezed out like a lemon. He hoped that when it was his time, he would give everything—be totally squeezed out for Soman. I think that's why he did what he did. He didn't just want to die from that poison. He wanted to give everything."

Raven nodded, looking down at her foot. "I wonder how I will die."

Franz chuckled. "John would tell you that is none of your business. The how and the wherefore are up to Soman. Your only business is staying on the path."

Raven nodded, her mind now lost in thought. She got up and went down into the ship's hold and stared at her old kite. It wasn't just coincidence that the *Eros* had come across it. She still had some part to play in this adventure.

CHAPTER 42

EVERY LAST DROP

SEVERAL DAYS LATER, THEY found themselves in calm waters. Redd and Tom were talking together along the side of the ship.

Franz nudged Raven. "What are they talking about?"

"They think we are close to a passageway they call the gate that leads to a strange land. Apparently it is guarded by some monster called Leviathan."

Franz nodded. "We have met. We didn't leave on the best of terms. I think he took it personally."

"Took what personally?"

"Me trying to carve out his eye."

Raven nodded. "I can see how he might take that personally."

"He's a monster. It's my job to kill him. It's what I do. It's not personal."

"I see. How will we know that he is near?"

Franz looked up at Raven. "The sea will boil, and it will feel like the end of the world. You'll know. That's not the problem. The problem is what you do about it."

Redd walked over and pointed to a shoreline in the distance, where a thin line of horizon shone through a narrow passage in what looked like a mountain that emptied into the sea. "That is the gate. *Eros* has brought us here before ... I think to take us through. But Levi will have none of it." He looked out over the sea. "She is out here somewhere."

It was then that Raven noted bubbles coming up from the ocean around them.

Redd yelled, "Hold on!"

A wind suddenly filled *Eros*'s sails, and she sped forward. Raven fell, having only one good leg to stand on. She looked down at her other leg, which she had put a long sock over. It was now black up to the knee. She could balance on it, but that was about it. The man in the forest had said she had about a week. Her week was up. She looked over to her right, and it seemed that an island was being formed before her eyes. A giant head then exploded into the heavens, followed by a neck that seemed to never end.

Redd was now handing out weapons to the crew, who were strapping up for battle. He looked over to Raven. "Her armor is too thick to do any serious damage. The only chance a man would have would be if he were to attack Levi from the inside." Redd shook his head and laughed. "But we fight anyway."

Raven sat for a moment, and then her eyes opened wide. She hobbled down to the ship's hold and found her kite sitting next to a barrel of water. She ran her hand across the smooth fabric. She then began to drag it up to the deck, but fell. She looked down at her bad leg, grabbed a nearby pole, and hit her leg with it. She felt nothing. She looked at the pole to see if she had broken it and found a small hand reaching down to her. She looked up to find a friendly face.

"Looks like you could use some help." Franz pulled Raven up to her feet.

Together they pulled the kite up to the deck of the ship. Raven looked out at Leviathan writhing through the air and the sea. There seemed to be no end to the beast. She lifted her head up as a stiff breeze hit her face.

Raven looked down at Franz. "It's a good breeze, but it's not enough to pick me up from so low. Somehow we need to get some height."

Franz smiled and held out a coil of rope.

Raven strapped herself in tight to the kite. Franz then tied the rope tight around her waist. He kicked her bad leg. "Every last drop."

Raven looked down and nodded.

Franz secured the rope onto the ship. Without warning, the wind pulled hard on *Eros*'s sails and she sped off. Raven stumbled backward several steps and off the back of the ship. Franz gave her a thumbs-up and slowly let out the rope. Raven sored higher and higher into the sky. When she was high enough, she pulled out her sword and cut the rope loose. *Eros* immediately banked hard right and headed straight for the gates.

The sea boiled with turbulent bubbles as Leviathan raced to the mountain to close off the pass. In moments she was next to the gates, but as if to taunt the men, she did not set her body in front of the gates. She raised her head high, ready to breathe fire on any who would risk that passage.

From high above, Raven watched these events unfold. In her heart, she felt a great warmth, and at that moment the kite sped off like the wind toward the gates. The wind whipped hard on her clothes as she passed over the *Eros*. Below she could see Redd pointing up at her. He waved, and she waved back as she sped by. The noise of the wind rushing by was deafening, and yet she could hear her sword humming out in front.

In the distance, she saw Leviathan's head. It swirled in the clouds, coming in and out of view. She then heard a voice like thunder.

"I see you, Raven. You will find no home beyond the gates." Leviathan blew a stream of fire that cut through the sky like lightning.

Raven banked hard right, barely evading the river of flame that passed her by. She then rose high in the air. Her legs now both hung limp and cold with no life in them. She dove into a cloud and for a moment was blinded by white. When she emerged, Leviathan was waiting for her. Levi's mouth blew flame as she dove straight down. The cloud behind her evaporated with a hiss.

"You are no more than a gnat to me, Raven. What end do you serve in your madness?" Leviathan then began to take in a big breath.

That was the moment Raven had been waiting for. She flew high into the sky, passing just by Leviathan. Her sword sliced through the tip of sea dragon's nostril. Leviathan's massive head tilted and sped forward in pursuit, but Raven moved faster as she rose. She could hear the air rush into the dragon's mouth as she readied herself to let loose flame. When the rush of her breath tapered to an end, Raven looped the kite around and began a breakneck descent straight toward Leviathan's head with her sword held firmly in front of her. Leviathan opened her mouth to let loose another river of flame. Raven passed through the mouth of the great beast and over her forked tongue. Raven's eyes watered from the sulfur in the air. In the span of a moment, she drove her sword hard into the back of the dragon's throat. She wore a smile on her face as she mouthed to herself, "Every last drop."

* * * * *

Redd looked up at watched as Raven flew straight into the mouth of Leviathan. He gasped in disbelief. Fire streamed from the dragon's mouth, followed by a howl of pain from the beast. The massive beast flailed wildly, roaring in agony.

With tears in his eyes, Redd watched as the *Eros* picked up speed. Leviathan lifted her head high to the heavens, and at that moment the wind picked up and shot the *Eros* through the gates. Through teary eyes, Redd beheld a sight more wondrous than he could have imagined.

Made in the USA
Monee, IL
25 July 2021